CW00525505

SWEETS FOR MY SWEET

SWEETS FOR MY SWEET

Janie Bolitho

This first world edition published in Great Britain 1996 by
SEVERN HOUSE PUBLISHERS LTD of
9–15 High Street, Sutton, Surrey SM1 1DF.
First published in the USA 1996 by
SEVERN HOUSE PUBLISHERS INC., of
595 Madison Avenue, New York, NY 10022.

British Library Cataloguing in Publication Data

Bolitho, Janie
    Sweets for My Sweet
    I. Title
    823.914 [F]

    ISBN 0-7278-4883-6

Typeset by Palimpsest Book Production Limited,
Polmont, Stirlingshire, Scotland.
Printed and bound in Great Britain by
Hartnolls Ltd, Bodmin, Cornwall.

Chapter One

Six thirty a.m. It was still dark outside, apart from the occasional flicker of an ailing streetlight. Alice shivered. It was cold in the flat, but not that cold. Lack of sleep, emotions worn ragged and a fear she was not sure was fully justified chilled her to the bone.

Friday morning. The last working day of the week but only another uncertain weekend to look forward to. So much had changed in the past couple of months. There was, she realised, just time for a bath. She ran the hot tap and steam filled the white, tiled room which she thought resembled a public lavatory more than a bathroom in a private flat. The fittings too, were solid, white porcelain, except for the greenish stains beneath the taps. In vivid contrast was the crimson gaudiness of the blooms of the Christmas Cactus on the windowsill and the succulent green of its stems against the paintwork.

The top half of Alice's small body was a reflected blur in the misted mirror as she stepped into the bath. She lay back, wetting her hair which was dark, almost black, and cut in wisps around her face. An elfin face, her father always said.

One telephone call doesn't amount to much, she told herself as the warmth seeped into her body. I'm being neurotic, and that's not like me.

1

Wanting to stay there longer, she made herself get out and, wrapped in a large towel, put the kettle on for coffee. While it boiled she put on underwear, socks, blouse, jeans, a warm jumper and boots. The uniform for work; uniform because the factory was chilly, cold underfoot even in the summer because the floor was concrete. All the women who worked there eventually gave in and put warmth before vanity. Alice smiled. All except Vera. The men had it easier because they were lifting and loading or worked near the warmth of the huge chocolate-processing vats, but in the summer the advantage was the women's; whilst the men sweated, they were cool.

Alice picked up her bag and keys and went downstairs in the still quiet house. She waved to the newsagent as he stacked his newspapers on the counter then rounded the corner into a gust of wind which sent an empty burger carton somersaulting ahead of her. Fifteen minutes later she was at the stop where the coach would pick her up. For those without cars the transport was free. Jack Winter knew how to look after his staff. Alice was one of the last to get on. Inside it was warm and smelled of wool and face powder and stale cigarettes. The new driver greeted her, showing off his recently acquired knowledge of their names. He was young, much younger than his predecessor and much more cheerful, and although he fancied his chances with some of the girls his thinness and greasy hair prevented his success.

She took a seat by a woman from accounts whom she hardly knew, to reduce the odds of having to make conversation. Vera had stared at her as she got on. Do I look that bad? she wondered as the coach pulled in through the open gates of Winter's Confectionery Company, now expanded to take up the whole of Weslar

2

Yard, and allowed the women, and one or two men, to disgorge noisily. Seven forty-five. There would be time for coffee. Sometimes they were later if they had to wait for a passenger.

Alice followed Vera and Marg into the cloakroom where they each had a locker for clothes and handbags. Vera went straight to the mirror to check that the corkscrews of highlighted, blonde hair were suitably dishevelled and her lipstick not smudged. As always, she was the only one wearing a skirt, a tight, black skirt.

"Are you OK?" She turned to look at Alice.

"No. I'm fed up. And I'm angry." It was true, anger had replaced fear now she was amongst other people.

"Keith again?" Vera's carmine lips were pursed in sympathy.

"I don't know what he's playing at. I've made it quite clear it's over."

"Coffee, you two?" Marg patted her hair and went off to make it.

"What's he done?" Vera asked as they followed Marg into the canteen.

"He rang me up in the middle of the night, that's what. Well, about one-thirty. I was asleep, it took me by surprise, I can't remember exactly what he said, something about getting me back."

"God, doesn't he ever give up?"

"Here." Marg placed the mugs on the scratched and scarred table. At fifty-four, but admitting to forty-nine, she was the oldest of their group. "Problems?" She studied Alice with a motherly expression thinking it was a shame that Alice had broken off her engagement to Keith. They had seemed well suited. Still, better now than later. But right before Christmas, it must have upset the boy a

3

great deal. But Alice was no silly teenager, she was twenty-four; old enough to know what she wanted out of life. "Men," she said in a tone which dismissed them all, after Alice told her about the phone call. "Here, look at the time, Jack'll be after us."

It was a paradox that although Jack Winter's company had expanded it now employed fewer staff than in the days of his father. Only the packing of the cellophane-wrapped boxes of chocolates was done by hand now. Technology, environmental health officers and EC directives had seen to that. Gone were the days when the individual chocolates came along on conveyor belts, the women's hands a blur as they sorted them, then filled the waiting boxes. When the extension was complete there would be a new canteen, replacing the room they now used which held tables and chairs, a large urn to make drinks, and a couple of snack and biscuit vending machines. Most of them prefered things the way they were because they often shopped in the lunch hour and simply used the seating to eat their sandwiches quickly before returning to work. The Asian contingency stuck together, huddling in the cloakroom with their Thermos flasks and Tupperware boxes, chattering away in Urdu, although they spoke English on the factory floor.

"Morning, ladies." Jack Winter smiled benevolently and rubbed his hands together, satisfied that several lorries were in the loading bay, the drivers collecting assignments of cream-filled or hard-centred chocolates, packaged in cellophane and sealed in cartons. He was under no misapprehensions: his firm was one of the best but just recently a smaller, rival company had begun manufacturing very similar products: not copying so closely he could take them to court for copyright

4

infringements, but near enough to tempt confuse retail customers with their slightly cheaper prices. Sales had dropped marginally; he had to ensure no further damage was done.

"Morning, Jack," his staff chorused back.

Alice stood at her allocated place and, as her hands moved automatically, she thought back again to her relationship with Keith. She had been the one to end it, two months ago, although before the final break she had tried hard to make Keith understand that their parting was inevitable unless he paid her more attention. She had always accepted that he needed a hobby, everyone did, but football and darts had begun to take up more and more of his time. His promise that Saturday nights would be *their* night for doing something together seemed to have been forgotten as more and more of them were spent at the social club, which was part of his sports club, until it had become routine. They might just as well have gone there on the Saturday of the Winter's Confectionery Christmas party, she thought. Keith had not danced with her once but had spent most of the evening standing at the bar talking football to someone's husband. It was then she had finally accepted what sort of life it would be if she married him; worse if they had had children, because she would be left on her own most evenings. Alice had ended it that night and no longer regretted the decision although she found the adjustment hard, after four years, being on her own again.

"It's time you found yourself another bloke," Vera said to her in the tea break. "Come out with us tonight."

"I might." Alice grinned. To Vera, a man was the answer to everything. Two husbands behind her and always a constant stream of suitors. Alice wondered how such a disparate group of women got on so well together.

That evening there was still some light in the sky when they finished work. Soon it would be spring. Already the buds of the daffodils in the park were turning from green to yellow. Alice had to decide what to do about the holiday she had booked in June which should have been her honeymoon.

Her face puckered in self-mockery as she trudged home realising it was Friday night with nowhere to go. She could not even pretend she was going to wash her hair as she had done it that morning, but she was not in the mood for an evening of Vera's lewdness and Marg's clichés. Perhaps Josie, downstairs, was free; they could get a few lagers or a bottle of wine and share a Chinese take-away. But Josie was going out. Up in her flat, Alice knew she had to pull herself together, that brooding over one stupid telephone call was ridiculous.

James Winter was Jack's middle child. He had inherited his mother's good looks and dress sense but his father's colouring. He was almost as dark as Alice Powell who worked on the shop floor. He knew her slightly, he knew them all slightly because he often went into the factory and he, like the rest of the family, was always present at the Christmas party. Jack insisted upon this and the staff liked him the more for it. He had watched them, Alice, and girls like her, and wondered how they could be so content with so little. Many were married, with children left with childminders, and there were others who could surely get more out of life than working for Winters' Confectionery Company. James, however, was able to look at and analyse the lives of others but unable to recognise his own shortcomings . . .

Tonight his parents were having friends around for dinner. Naturally, he had been invited, but he did not want to be the odd one out now that he and Kate had parted. He wasn't really sorry; Kate had been more his mother's choice than his; yet another daughter of a local well-to-do family whom his parents encouraged him to meet. One day he would have to settle down, marry a girl he could get along with if not love, but she would need to be a very understanding sort of female . . .

James stood in front of the full length mirrors which lined one wall of his bedroom and formed the doors of his wardrobes. He selected jockey shorts, socks and a neatly-folded shirt. From another section he took a pair of trousers from their hanger. His naked body, he thought, as he surveyed it, wasn't bad although his legs were not as muscled as he would have liked. He dressed and combed his wet hair but even before he splashed on some aftershave with the palms of his hands, the tang of it lingered in the room from the time when he had knocked a bottle off the dressing-table. Fortunately it had not stained the Wilton carpet but the scent had permeated the fibres and was a constant reminder of a temper not always under control.

He shrugged his arms into a jacket and went down-stairs to wait for his taxi. "The Chicago Bar, please," he instructed the driver when it arrived. Through the misted windows he watched as it began to rain, large drops bouncing off the elongated bonnet of the car. Red and green neon flashed across the windscreen and, momentarily, in that light the driver's hands looked like dead, lifeless things as they rested on the wheel.

7

Tonight he was meeting Larry. He did not always treat Larry well, ignoring him for days on end, but in a perverse sort of way he needed him. Larry had a habit of doing things of which Ruth and Jack Winter would not approve and for this reason his name had never been mentioned at home. James had to admit he did not always approve himself but there was something about Larry he was unable to resist, and it was too late to call a halt now. Besides, he had been with him since his schooldays and you did not abandon old friends. Occasionally, if he tried very hard, James could be strong and control Larry, prevent trouble, but it took an enormous amount of willpower.

The town was busy. Friday night busy. The rain, now falling like stair-rods, was not going to spoil anyone's fun. Buses and cars and taxis swished through the water already lying in the gutters, pubs doors opened and closed letting out light and noise and cigarette smoke into the streets. A weekend feeling was in the air.

The Chicago Bar was not a pub, it was more of a cocktail lounge and attached to an hotel and restaurant. Behind the counter rows of bottles gleamed, reflected in the glass against which they rested. Diamonds of light winked over surfaces as the Twenties style crystal globes revolved overhead. To complete the image the barman wore a patterned waistcoat, a black bow-tie and armbands to hold up his sleeves.

James ordered a whisky sour. It was happy hour, so he got two for the price of one. He laughed aloud at the idea Larry had come up with and wondered why he hadn't thought of it himself. The barman, polishing glasses, watched James in the mirrored wall and gave a shrug of resignation. He had come across him before.

The reason James had not come up with Larry's idea was that although they were close, they did not think alike, and he had not expected Larry to turn up at the Christmas party. As always, many of Jack's employees had had too much to drink and the place had been crowded as everyone was permitted to bring a guest so Larry's presence had not been noticeable to anyone but himself.

Because the idea now seemed like a good one, James had forgotten his initial annoyance and disgust when Larry sneered, saying these women were nothing, that they were boring and stupid. He had pointed at Vera Langford, sniggering at her tight mini-dress, then at Marg Finch who, he said, must believe herself to be some sort of Fifties sex symbol with her out of date hair-style and too much visible cleavage.

Strange he had not said anything about Alice Powell, but what was there to say? She was young and pretty and seemed more intelligent than the rest of them. James liked her and wished he had the nerve to ask her out. The last girl he had dated had lost interest after several weeks and finally ditched him after two months. He was awkward in women's company, unsure how to behave because he was unsure of what they expected or wanted from a man. His mother had been the only stable female in his life: calm, unflappable Ruth; not that he particularly wished for a girlfriend like that, he just wanted someone who was capable of understanding him.

He knew he ought not to have been drinking that night at the Christmas party, at least, not as much as he had done. It was then, taking advantage of his weakness, that Larry had made the suggestion and James had not had the strength to resist. Then Jack, noticing his son's condition had taken him to one side and had a quiet word, telling him that if he did not know how to behave he should not have come at all. The next thing James remembered was being put into a taxi and taken home.

But that was then. Best forgotten. He ordered another drink, and one for Larry. He always knew just when Larry was about to put in an appearance.

Only fleetingly did he wonder why his father seemed less his cheerful, easy-going self. James had other things on his mind.

Jack Winter smiled at his wife. He was a lucky man, Ruth was beautiful and he loved her and there had been a time when he might have lost her. She hardly suffered now from the crippling shyness which had made her youth a misery. He poured them both a drink, knowing just how little brandy and just how much soda she liked. One drink was enough to take the edge off the anxiety she experienced when they were having people for dinner. Her uncertainty was beyond his comprehension. Apart from her looks she had the gift of being a good conversationalist and knew instinctively how to entertain, but he possessed more than enough confidence for both of them, occasionally, he was told, to the point of being brash.

They were both dressed ready for the evening, Ruth in a mustard slub silk dress which should have clashed with, but instead enhanced, the colouring of her reddish hair. Jack was in a suit for once, instead of one of the rather flamboyant checked jackets he favoured.

Ruth, he reflected, had even been unsure with the children when they were small, always wondering if she was doing the right thing – even though she had

had three of them. Ironically, now they were older there was a stronger bond between them and their mother than he had encountered in other families.

"Jack? What're you thinking?" Ruth frowned in concern. He had mentioned one or two problems at work but had not been specific.

"Sorry, love. A competitor's after our share of the market. Nothing too much to worry about at the moment, but I want to nip it in the bud. *How* is the problem. Still, we're up and running with the Easter Eggs." He grinned. "And only a couple of people know how they're going to be packaged. Things'll pick up, you'll see."

"I know. It's you I worry about, not the factory. I wish James would take an interest, it's not good for him, drifting about as he does."

"He might. Eventually. When he finds himself a wife. Responsibility changes young men."

Ruth looked away. To her it seemed an unlikely proposition although the right woman might be the solution to her son's problems. At least Polly was doing well, happily married and teaching in a school for children with special needs. Simon, the baby of the family, was still studying history at university, but he had already made it quite clear that he was not interested in continuing the family dynasty. "Let James have it," he said frequently. Simon's interest was in things past, not the future.

"They're here." Jack had heard their guests' car on the gravel of the drive.

Marjorie Finch plodded down Chapel Street with two bulging carrier bags. She always did the weekend shopping on her way home on Fridays because she liked to get her hair done on Saturday mornings. In her black boots and red coat, her large-boned face topped with a Marilyn Monroe hairstyle, she was an impressive, if breathless figure. Her lodger, Mr Green, had been watching from the window and came out to relieve her of the plastic bags. "Evening, Marg," he said.

Bless him, she thought. He had been with her for eleven years, ever since her husband, Monty, had died and she had needed the money to keep on the 'two up, two down' terraced house they had been in the process of buying. Monty had also worked at the factory, had done so in Jack's father's time, back in the days of the blast furnaces when he was a stoker. Stripped to the waist, sweating, he had been a fine-looking man and full of life. But after a couple of months it was not only Monty who had been full of life and the register office wedding had been hastily arranged.

Marg had not exactly hitched up her skirts and danced when he died, but neither did she grieve. Monty had been a drinker. The heat from the furnaces, he claimed, gave him a thirst which he quenched in the pub which, in turn, had led to an enlarged liver, shortly followed by his funeral. Mr Green had no such tendencies.

He was, Marg realised, a bit of a loner, enjoying his job and his quiet hobbies but never really socialising. He had only accompanied her to the Christmas party because he felt it would have been rude to refuse the invitation. He wasn't too bad to look at and, as far as she knew, had no disgusting habits. Strange he had never married. But perhaps he had – he had just said he was single when he had applied for the room; maybe he was divorced. It was too late to make inquiries after all these years.

Mr Green made a pot of tea while Marg put away

the groceries and saw to their meal. The potatoes were peeled, as they were every Friday night when Mr Green finished early down at the timber yard.

"I'm meeting Vera tonight," Marg told him.

"Does you good to get out. I don't like to see you overdoing things. Shall I leave you some supper out?"

"No, don't bother." She did not say that after several glasses of gin and orange she never felt like eating and Mr Green disapproved of anything in excess. He was a tidy man, she had to give him that. His bedroom was always neat and he hung up his anorak the moment he came through the door. Nor was she forever falling over shoes as she had done in Monty's time.

"You look a picture," he said when she came downstairs after changing to go out. Black shoes, a black skirt and an emerald jumper with a wide rib had replaced her working clothes. Her figure could only be described as statuesque; wide shoulders, a large bosom and hips, but still a clearly-defined waist, even if it measured half as much again as it once had. In her younger days, Mr Green thought, she must've been a stunner.

In the Ladies at the back of The Unicorn pub, Vera swayed this way and that in front of the mirror. "Do you think I'm putting on weight?" she asked. She scooped up the mass of her hair with both hands to see if it made any difference.

"Putting on weight? You're like a matchstick, you are. Turn sideways and they'd mark you absent," Marg replied.

"Thanks, Marg, you can always be relied upon to boost a girl's confidence."

"Some girl. Come on, my gin's getting warm."

Back at their table they gossiped about work, both

commenting that there seemed to be something up with Alice, something more than just finishing with Keith. "She'll tell us if she wants to. Best leave things alone," Marg concluded.

"I expect you're right." Vera spoke with one eye on the two men propped up at the bar, who were looking her way. The neckline of her leotard top left little to the imagination. "Still, where's there's men, there's trouble."

"You'd know, if anyone did. Mr Green's not so bad. He's offered to run me down to the coast on Sunday if the weather's not too bad."

"You and your Mr Green."

"He's not *my* Mr Green, Vera, there's no need for sarcasm. I keep telling you our relationship is totally platonic. Not everyone jumps into bed with every man they meet."

"If only," Vera grinned. It was infectious. Marg shook her head, smiling back. There was only one Vera.

"Come on, one more drink then I'm going home. I suppose you're staying?" Marg queried, nodding in the direction of the bar.

"Too right. Too good a chance to miss."

"You're an opportunist strumpet, that's what you are Vera Langford."

"You and your long words. Go on, mine's a vodka."

When Marg had left Vera went to refill her glass. The two men at the bar made room for her. "Hello, Vera. All right?"

"I'm fine."

"Let me get that for you."

"Cheers." Greg Rawlins was unlike most of the men

she had been out with. He liked a good time but he was less raucous about it, and he was certainly nothing like her two husbands. The first one had been a mistake – on both their parts. They had rushed into it, too young to appreciate their differences, but the second time, she had to admit, was her fault for not knowing better. He had always been rough – playfully rough, she assumed, and she liked men who were strong. Then he had slapped her. Just the once, and there had been apologies and promises of it never happening again. Less than a month later it had, and this time the slap was more of a blow. After a year she had had enough and had thrown him out. It had not been easy to get rid of him because she had no family to back her up: no brothers, only a sister in Scotland to whom she had not spoken for several years and parents who had given up on her long before.

She could not imagine Greg to be capable of hurting anyone. And certainly not her; no one got near Vera Langford any more. She had learned her lesson long ago.

Chapter Two

Liz Powell came to the door with a tea towel in her hand. "Hi, how's things?"

"Fine." Alice kissed her mother. This small reassurance did little to alleviate Liz's concern for her daughter.

"Is Dad in?"

"Not yet. He's having a quick drink; he won't be long. I told him what time luch would be ready."

"I'm not sure I'm very hungry."

"Of course you are. You must eat. I'm sure you don't look after yourself properly."

"All mothers say that."

Liz saw a flash of humour in Alice's face and hoped the stubborness she had inherited from herself would get her through this quickly. Liz liked Keith, liked him very much, but she refused to interfere in Alice's life. "Here's Dad now," she said, hearing Derek's key in the lock.

Alice had been persuaded to have Sunday lunch at home. On Saturday she had cleaned the flat and bought food. Whilst in the town centre she had window-shopped and been tempted by a russet pinafore dress and the tan T-shirt artfully displayed beneath it. It now hung in her wardrobe.

Derek Powell came into the kitchen and ruffled his daughter's hair as he sniffed appreciatively at the rich aroma of roasting lamb. He smelled of soap and after-shave, just as the bathrooom did because it was stocked with samples he got from his job as a rep for a cosmetics and toiletries firm. Alice, too, benefitted from this. Between them, the Powells did all right. Liz worked behind the counter of a butcher's in the precinct and got a good discount, if not free meat.

They sat down to eat and to prevent discussion of her present situation Alice picked up her knife and fork and surprised herself by clearing her plate. Derek gave Liz a gratified wink as she cleared the kitchen table. The dining-room, since Alice and Mark had left, had become more of a storeroom and sewing room for Liz and was only used on special occasions.

"Has Keith been in touch again?" Liz asked when Alice was leaving. Alice wanted to walk off the meal before it was dark and, later, she was going to the cinema with Josie.

"No." It was not strictly a lie. The more she thought about it the less certain she was it was Keith's voice she had heard on the telephone at one-thirty, last Friday morning.

"Get in touch on Wednesday. Or pop over. You know we love to see you any time," her mother said.

"I will. 'Bye. And thanks for the lunch, it was lovely."

A frost which fell during the night surprised everybody after two days of rain. The pavements had dried about midnight and when Alice pulled back the bedroom curtains on Monday morning the tops of the cars in the street and the roofs of the houses opposite were coated with a thin, glittering film.

The phone call, as threatening as it had seemed at the time, was more or less forgotten. Now she concentrated on keeping her hands warm as she made her way to the bus-stop. Lights were on in most houses as people got ready for work or for school. Here and there a television screen flickered behind an uncurtained window. Alice hoped her feet would not feel like blocks of ice before she even got to work. She pulled the collar of her coat up around her neck. It was her Christmas present from her parents, thick and navy, with wide revers and large buttons and the classiest item of clothing she owned. It was a shame to wear it to work but the weather demanded it. Keith's present to her – gold ear-rings, which had been already wrapped and under the Powell's tree, had been returned unopened despite his protests she should keep them.

He was still so often on her mind but she knew, in time, it would pass. What a pair, she thought, relieved to see the coach at the traffic lights. At least I finally made a move. Keith still lived with his mother. That, of course, had been another problem.

"Mum needs me," he used to say, which made her wonder what was going to happen when they were married. There was always the niggling doubt that they would be expected to live with her. Keith's father had died many years ago and his older, married brother lived some three hundred miles away. It had always irritated Alice the way Joan Wenton manipulated her son and made no effort to build a new life of her own.

Alice took the vacant seat in front of Marg and Vera. "Never again," Marg was saying. "I know I've said it before, but this time I mean it. Mr Green and I are going away next year."

18

"She's still on about Christmas," Vera informed Alice.

"You weren't there, my girl, you've no idea what it's like to be treated like a doormat by your own family. And poor Mr Green spent most of the time in his room."

"*His* room?" Vera asked.

"Vera, how many times have I told you —"

"Only teasing. No need to get in a strop."

Marg stared huffily out of the window but could not keep it up for long. She sniffed and patted her hair. "How did it go on Friday? After I left you?"

"It was great. You ought to have stayed and we could've made up a foursome. Unless, of course, Mr Green would've objected."

"Vera!"

Alice grinned. Poor Marg. But no one really knew what the relationship was between her and her lodger.

"Greg," Vera was saying, "that's the one with the fair hair, took me on to a club." She stopped and chewed a lip which was a deep pink, the colour bleeding into the fine lines around her mouth. "Funny that, he said he'd ring on Sunday."

"You mean your hundred per cent record's broken?"

"It's not that, Marg. It was weird, someone did ring, but I'm sure it wasn't Greg. I didn't listen properly at first, thinking it was him. All I got was a bit about women like me getting what they deserved. Then they hung up. But I can't think who else it could be."

Marg raised a black-pencilled eyebrow and snorted. "Come off it, girl, there can't be many men in this town who don't have your number."

Alice swivelled around in her seat. Coincidence? Probably, Vera did know an awful lot of men. But there were faint shadows under her eyes as if it had caused her a restless night, and that was not like Vera. "Perhaps it's the same person."

"What person?" Vera was puzzled.

"The same as whoever rang me. On Thursday night. Don't you remember, I told you about it?"

"God, I hope not, that's too creepy for my liking."

"How well do you know this bloke, Greg?" Marg asked.

Vera shrugged. "How well do you ever know anyone? I met him about six months ago when he was drowning his sorrows because his divorce had come through. I told him he ought to be celebrating. I've seen him a couple of times since. He seems all right. As far as men go, that is. In fact," she admitted, "he's quite nice."

"Vera Langford, I do believe you're blushing."

Vera turned away but they had reached the factory and began trooping across the forecourt to the main entrance.

It was a busy day, made more hectic when one of the mixing machines broke down. Jack stalked about cursing the machine, the men who operated it and the manufacturers but no one took any notice. None of his insults was personal and he would calm down just as quickly.

"All right, girls, have a tea break," he said. "Ten minutes, no more, it'll be fixed by then." Then, hopefully he would be free to go over the figures again. An idea had occurred to him, a way of dealing with the bothersome opposition, but it required more looking into before it was safe to go ahead.

The fork-lift truck drivers trundled over to collect the boxes of Easter Eggs, piled high against the back wall. Marg went off to make tea, sniffing disdainfully when one of the men loading the eggs winked at her.

It was more than fifteen minutes before Jack came in to say they could go back to work and, having enjoyed an extra break, the day seemed to pass quickly. Only Alice seemed aware that recently a small furrow, hardly ever visible, had become a permanant feature across Jack's forehead.

Later, they were meeting in The Unicorn. It was a pub they favoured because it was both central and lively. One of the girls was leaving to get married and Monday night was the only time she could spare for her hen night as she was moving away from the area.

"See you at eight," Vera called as Alice got off the coach.

Alice decided to wear her new pinafore; new clothes always cheered her up. When she arrived at The Unicorn Vera was already there in leopard-skin leggings, black top and dangling silver ear-rings. Alice joined her at the table she had reserved – a large, round one in the corner.

The bride-to-be and several others came in, then Marg, resplendent in a violet satin skirt and a mauve top which flowed over her solid bulk. Her platinum hair, with the wave over one eye, was stiff with lacquer. As she was still standing she was sent to the bar. For all her size she was light on her feet, her movements graceful and the plump, pink hands carrying the tray were capable and safe.

At closing time, when Alice got a taxi home, she realised it was the first time for months she had really enjoyed herself. Laughter had come spontaneously.

She let herself in through the front door and climbed the one flight of steps to her flat, her key already in her hand. She switched on the light and glanced around. It was basic, but it was home now she had added her own bits and pieces. There were daffodils in a jug, purchased, three bunches for a pound, from a man in the street who appeared every year during February and March, and over the back of the worn settee she had thrown a brightly coloured rug. She could smell the apples she had bought and which, if she didn't eat soon, would go rotten.

Only when she turned to put on the table lamp did she see that a note had been pushed through the door in her absence. *'Your telephone's been ringing all evening. I hope it's nothing urgent. Love Josie,'* it read.

Quarter to twelve. Alice's mouth was dry. She dialled her parents' number, they were in bed but not asleep. "No, it wasn't us, love," her mother said.

Alice double-checked the door and the windows before she went to bed. For an hour she lay waiting for it to ring again and finally dropped off into an uneasy sleep.

Initially Keith Wenton had not taken Alice's outburst at the Christmas party seriously. It had been late; the party had not finished until two, she was tired or had had too many glasses of wine, he had thought. In retrospect he realised how many other occasions there had been when he had let her down.

"She'll get over it," his mother had said, "give her a few days and she'll've forgotten all about it." But Joan Wenton, certain that anyone who got her son would never give him up, was wrong.

Keith had tried telephoning, calling round and had even resorted to writing to tell Alice how he felt, but she had been adamant: as far as she was concerned, it was over.

After Christmas, when he was back at work, it had been easier. There was not much time to brood but he was still determined they would be together again. They belonged together. A month, he had decided. A month would be long enough for her to start missing him. But at the end of January nothing had changed and then one more month had elapsed.

It was strange, for all his mother's dependence and her endless hypochondriacal complaints, she too was disappointed that the engagement was off. But Joan Wenton had her own reasons . . .

One evening, at the beginning of March, Keith called at the Powells' house on his way home.

"Keith, come in. How nice to see you."

Liz studied him over a cup of coffee. He had lost weight, his features were sharper but when he smiled, the pointed incisors showing wickedly, he was the same old Keith. He was solid, hard-working and loyal and these attributes, Liz guessed, were partly responsible for his downfall. All right, he had been inattentive at times, but he would never have let Alice down. It was, Liz realised from experience, the bastards you really fell for.

"Yes," she said, "I'm sorry, love," when he asked if she believed Alice was certain of what she was doing.

He left then; there was nothing more to say. He went out into the street and unlocked the door of the van which belonged to the electricity board for whom he worked and which was another reminder of what he had lost. He had met Alice through her brother, Mark, who was also an electrician.

In the town centre the traffic was at a standstill. A dual carriageway bisected the main shopping area, guarded by metal barriers to prevent pedestrians risking their lives. Bus-stops lined one side but the buses caused more delays because of the cars parked in the marked-out bays. The pavements here were very wide with trees to break up the concrete monotony. The buds were just visible. Here too, were the frontages of the large stores found in every town, closed now but their window displays lit to tempt the late pedestrians.

The lights changed twice before Keith was able to get through them. He ran an impatient hand through his hair which was nearer blond than brown, and neatly shaped. Alice had not liked it when it was spiked on top. I've tried everything, he thought, but there has to be a way to make her come back to me.

"What's up girls?" Jack Winter, in a jacket comprising maroon and black squares divided by thin yellow lines surveyed the subdued group of women. Even the local radio station which normally blared out all day over the sounds of machinery was turned down low. The glare of the fluorescent tubes suspended between the overhead girders of the superstructure was less than kind to their complexions. And then he grinned. "Of course," he said. "Beverley's hen night. I hope it was worth it."

"Bugger off, Jack." Vera sashayed over to the collection point, her hair, in a band on top of her head, swaying in time with her hips.

Jack shook his head and went back to his office which was reached by a short flight of metal steps and from which, through the glass-sided top half he could see most of the factory. It was something which gave him pleasure, to be able to look down and know it was all his. His alone. No board of directors to answer to, no bank breathing down his neck, and better still, he was giving employment to many people. The town had been good to his family; he was repaying the debt. Admittedly

24

he also enjoyed the kudos his position gave him and the doors it had opened. He was, however, ashamed to admit, even to himself, that he also relished the envy that people who claimed to be his friend were unable to disguise.

Alice. He observed her as she worked. Even paler than she had been of late. It was strange how he felt about her. No, best not to think about it, such thoughts were not part of this Jack Winter's world, the Jack Winter who had turned near failure into success. And who was fighting to hold on to that success.

Alice let herself in and checked the hall table for post. One circular. The bills were not due for a few weeks yet. Upstairs she drew the curtains, then stretched out her legs in front of the electric fire to warm her feet. In a minute, when she could be bothered, she would make something to eat. There was some mince in the fridge. Last night had been fun but she had paid the penalty this morning when another couple of hours sleep would have been welcome. It would be an early night tonight.

It can't be Keith, she thought, recalling how upset Marg had been, on top of a hangover. Marg had said she was hardly in the door when the telephone rang:

"Mr Green was in bed asleep. It must've been getting on for twelve. All I could think of was that something had happened to one of the kiddies." She did not mention the overwhelming guilt as she recalled how she had berated her children and grandchildren over Christmas. "It was awful." Marg repeated the words verbatim:

" 'You're a slut,' the voice had said, 'a fornicating slut. You and that lodger of yours. You'll pay for it, you'll see.' "

"I stood with the receiver in my hand for ages," she

said. "I couldn't believe it, and I can't even say if it was a man or a woman."

"It's someone who knows us," Vera had replied. "It has to be: they knew about Mr Green, Marg, and my, well, men, and whoever rang Alice pretended to be Keith."

Alice went over it all again. What could anyone possibly have against them? They had wondered if Stella Roberts was responsible. She had joined the firm some weeks ago and kept to herself. If she did speak it was only to let them know she was used to better things, that factory work was beneath her. And there were times Alice caught her watching them, especially if they were fooling around, and there was unconcealed malice in her eyes. It was Vera who had found out she was divorced. Perhaps she was bitter, not able to bear anyone else enjoying themselves. But how could they ask? A question could be answered with a lie; an outright accusation could get them into trouble. The only hope was that Stella, if it was her, had now got it out of her system.

"Damn it!" Alice said aloud as she went out to the tiny kitchen. "There's no point in worrying about it."

She sliced an onion, forgetting, as always, to do so under running water. Her eyes streamed but the anticipation of chilli and rice made up for it as the onion rings sweated gently in the pan. Once the meat was browned and simmering she turned the gas down low and checked the evening paper to see what was on television. There was nothing she wanted to watch. It was time, she decided, to do something with her life. Tomorrow she would rejoin the leisure centre and, when the new term started, find an evening class to suit her. She had become lazy, socialising only with the women with whom she worked. She had forgotten many of her friends had really been Keith's friends.

She undressed and put on the pink towelling dressing gown which swamped her slender figure, then switched on the radio. The easy-cook rice took only a few minutes. Her meal was on the table when the telephone rang. "Hello?" she said.

"Alice, it's me. I want you back, I'll do anything if you'll come back to me."

She slammed down the receiver so hard it fell off its rest. So it was Keith. And he was trying to get at her by getting at her friends. How dare he! The sight of her meal made her feel sick.

She was half dressed again before she realised that to go rushing over to tell him what she thought was just what he wanted, but she was not prepared to live with Keith's veiled threats hanging over her. When her anger had subsided was the time to speak to him. Finally she managed to eat then picked up a library book. The written word always soothed her.

Later, peering from behind the corner of the curtain at her bedroom window, Alice watched a few late-night passers-by. It was noisier here than at her parents' house. The newsagent stayed open until ten because he had a liquor licence and hired out videos; there was a pub on the corner, and, the kebab house. Three youths were just coming out of it, spilling fatty meat as they ate from the paper wrapping. Coming from the opposite direction, and presumably from the pub, was an elderly man who was allowing his dog to take him home. Out there, she realised, were so many people with their lives and their problems, most of which would be worse than hers.

Lulled by the sounds of the night she fell asleep.

*   *   *

27

During James Winter's miserable schooldays Larry had been a great comfort. He had hated boarding school and, unable to fit in, some of the children had been cruel to him. His parents did not know; he had not wanted them to think him weak. Yet they would have removed him and sent him to the local comprehensive if he had told them. Jack was no snob, he had simply believed he was doing the best for his children, and his other son Simon had loved it at the school.

Higher education had been out of the question: James had decided that he was never again going to be part of a large establishment. His aversion to groups meant he also had a very small social circle, his few girlfriends not really of his own choosing. His looks were no deterrent: olive-skinned and dark haired, he was attractive to women, and his eyes, not hazel, but deep brown, made them want to know what went on behind them.

James shrugged. Larry would be waiting. He put on jeans and a leather jacket. Tonight they were going to what he called, 'slum it'. His father would have a fit if he knew some of the dives they drank in; places where drugs were no secret and where prostitutes hung out. James liked to imagine he was seeing life. He was simply bored.

One of his problems, he knew, was that he couldn't settle. His parents had tried hard to find things he might enjoy doing. There was nothing wrong with his brain, he learned easily. It was just that once he'd accomplished the skill of a new interest, he lost the impetus to continue with it. Oddly enough, he wasn't like that with women; it was the converse. Whatever form the relationship took, it was always they who ended it.

At least he still had Larry. James was astute enough to realise he would never meet a female suitable to marry in any of the establishements they frequented, but it was fun, a part of his life that no one else knew about.

Strange he should be thinking of Alice when he had this evening to look forward to. Perhaps tomorrow he would call in at the factory; he would at least try to gauge her reaction to him. And the machinery fascinated him. As a child Jack had taken him in and he would watch for hours as the conveyor belts jerked and rumbled. And how the women had spoiled him, feeding him chocolates that his father said he must not have. One or two of the same women still worked there, although they were now nearing retirement age. The younger ones were different. He could not imagine them turning into motherly, middle-aged women. They were confident and knew their rights. At least they had a good boss.

The bar was basic. Varnished floorboards from which cigarette ends were easily swept, no stools at the counter and only a few tables and chairs. The people who came here wanted drink, not meals or quiet conversation or entertainment, and the beer was cheap. Strangely enough, there was rarely any trouble; only once that he could recall and that had been Larry's fault. He had been threatened with being barred but had gone back and apologised and the landlord had said all right, as long as he didn't upset any of his customers again.

"A bitter top, please," James said, smiling, hoping the barman did not remember the incident.

His smile widened. Larry was there.

Chapter Three

The next day the atmosphere at the factory was less tense and the radio was once more on full blast. Often, to relieve the monotony of their work, they sang along to the songs they knew. Vera, perhaps because she was less inhibited, had the loudest and best voice although Alice could hold a tune. Marg growled flatly, unaware, or unconcerned that the sounds she made were a little harsh on the ear, but they were lost amongst the other noises.

James Winter had been wandering around for most of the morning and they assumed his frequent visits were to learn the business. Jack often spoke of his children but it had sometimes crossed their minds that he had never mentioned exactly what James did for a living.

Sometimes James shut himself up with Jack's secretary, Phyllis, in her small office next to his own, and they would hear laughter, which surprised them because Phyllis had never been seen to smile in front of any of them. In a way it was understandable: they had heard the gossip and if it was true, she did not have much to smile about.

James stopped and watched the women. They were united by their work and their singing and he knew he would never be part of anything similar. Unembarrassed by his presence, especially the older women who had known him since boyhood, they continued to sing until the record ended and the news was being read. James walked off without a word and climbed the stairs to his father's office.

Vera came back from the lunch break with a half-pleased, half-anxious expression. She had been into town and bought a new nightdress which she pulled from the bag to show them.

"Bloody hell, girl, that'll hardly cover the essentials," Marg commented wryly. "A new man, I take it?"

But Vera did not answer, although she seemed to be on some sort of high, because later, coming back from the collection point she said, "And now, ladies, let's see what's on the agenda today." It was a perfect mimicry of Jack Winter.

"Ve-ra," Alice hissed, then pressed her lips together to stop herself from laughing.

"Now this," Vera continued, swinging to one side exactly in the way Jack did, "is," she stopped, her eyes wide, when she saw, a couple of feet behind her, one arm folded cupping the opposite elbow, his hand over his mouth, the very man she was imitating.

"Much more of that Vera Langford—" but he did not complete his sentence either. Marg's shoulders, under several layers of jumpers, heaved, and Alice lowered her eyes so he would not see the laughter in them. Good, he thought, she's recovering. Perhaps now it'll work out all right. Pulling himself up to his five feet nine inches he went back to his office. His back, in the black and white dog-tooth jacket was an accusation in itself. But they had all seen the twitch of his lips and his own suppressed mirth.

The afternoon wore on and Alice became quieter,

knowing what she had to do as soon as she left work. "I won't be on the coach," she told Marg, not wanting to delay them in waiting for her.

At five, she pulled on her jacket and headed towards the factory gates. A car tooted. Only when it tooted again did she glance around. There at the kerb was James Winter, smiling and beckoning her over. Without make-up and her hair ruffled by the breeze, Alice looked about seventeen, but her surprise was genuine when James asked if he could take her out the following night.

"Yes," she said, "I'd like that." And the arrangements were made before it had really sunk in.

It seemed only seconds before she reached the dual carriageway. Eyeing the traffic she knew she would have to go out of her way and use the subway. The pedestrian lights were useless at this time of day as cars jumped the lights or queued on the yellow diamonds of the box junctions. The noise of their engines reverberated as she went through the tunnel.

Joan Wenton felt the beginnings of a headache. The dullish throb in her temples would increase until it became a tight band around her head making it impossible to concentrate on anything else. She smoothed down the grey skirt which hung loosely from the waist and straightened the hem of her cardigan. Everything that she wore was clean and pressed but was chosen for neatness and warmth rather than style or fashion. Joan was short and of average build, except for the slackness of her stomach muscles which made her appear dumpy. Her features were on the coarse side, open-pored, and she had given up going to the hairdresser after her husband had died. But none of these things worried her. What did worry her was Keith. And Alice.

Joan would never admit it but she would have preferred her son to remain single until she was in her grave. Failing that, Alice was the next best thing. She was malleable and would have taken little persuasion to move into the Wenton household. Joan's arguments had been well rehearsed: it would be cheaper, there would be no housework or cooking for Alice and, when the time came, they would have a ready-made babysitter. Alice was always polite and respectful. Joan had mistaken this for lack of strength and confidence. Liz and Derek Powell could have told her otherwise; even at her most stubborn Alice could still remain polite.

In the oblong kitchen with its outdated appliances, Joan ran the tap and filled a glass with cold water before swallowing two painkillers. Keith was bound to notice how ill she looked and offer to stay in. He had taken to going out again lately, and that was another worry. She was terrified he would meet another girl; one who would take him away from her. For that reason she had to help him try to get Alice back.

Keith's mouth was in a grim line when he came in from work, it was not the time to broach the subject, besides, her head was splitting.

It was not only Alice on Keith's mind; he was sick of his mother's complaining, sick of her platitudes, her hackneyed sentiments, all spoken without thought. He was also sick of the endless routine and the 'meat and two vegetables' meals which were promptly produced every evening. Knowing he was going to marry Alice had made it bearable but she had not been an excuse to get away, he loved her. He still loved her. Her impish face when she grinned, her sense of humour, her small bones felt through her flesh when he picked her up, these things he could not get out of his mind. A knock at the door interrupted his thoughts.

"You get it," Joan said as she strained cabbage.

"Alice." It was no more than a croak. Keith's mouth was dry, his heart thumping. "Come in."

"No. I'm sick to death of your telephone calls, I'm sick of you pestering me all hours of the day and night. Leave me alone, do you hear, or I shall go to the police."

"I've rung . . . Alice . . . but not in the night. I wouldn't do that."

"Just stop it." And with that she was gone, walking very quickly up the street to hide the tears she had not been expecting.

Keith was motionless, unable to follow her, unable to think. Slowly he shut the front door and turned around. Joan stood in the hallway with a saucepan in her hand.

"Well, really," she said. "What a nerve."

It had been quite a day. Alice was hardly able to take it all in. All the carefully thought out things she had intended to say to Keith had gone out of her mind when she had confronted him, but at least the message must be clear now. Only when she had shut her door behind her did she allow herself to think about James.

They had discussed him at work, just as they did all the Winter family and it was unanimously agreed he was good looking. But he was the boss's son, so that was as far as it went. "I wouldn't say no," had been Vera's contribution. And tomorrow night she, Alice, was going out with him. She had, she realised, forgotten to rejoin the leisure centre on her way home, but the nervous

34

excitement had been building up. It was four years since she had been out with anyone but Keith.

Unable to decide what she would really like to eat Alice put a jacket potato in the oven. That would do for a start. When the telephone rang she answered it without hesitation. It was Wednesday; it would be her mother.

"Alice. Oh, dear, Alice, you're going to pay for what you've done."

"Who?" she began. But the line was dead.

Stella Roberts knew the other women didn't like her. They talked about her behind her back. Laughed at her. It was not her fault she happened to speak nicely, nor was it her fault she was reduced to such circumstances. When her husband had finally left her she had had no idea he was in debt, that he was hocked up to the hilt and that she was to be left with nothing. Their nice house had had to go, repossessed by the building society and she, Stella Roberts, could no longer hold up her head. Thankfully she had been rehoused on the other side of town and no longer saw their old friends.

What hurt most was that the children didn't seem to care. She had brought them up nicely. "Good manners and respectability count for more in life than anything else," she had told them frequently. But lately she saw she might as well have saved her breath. Martin, the older by three years, had jumped at the chance to leave school before taking his 'A' Levels and Rebecca, now at the local comprehensive, was a disgrace, with her uniform all over the place, chewing gum, and her speech, it made Stella cringe to listen to it. Worse, was that Stella knew she could have dealt with it, sorted out the problems if she did not have to spend nine hours, apart from lunchtime, packing chocolates because she had no qualifications for anything else, because her husband had led her to believe she would never need to work.

She glanced a few feet to her right, which was as far as she could get from the other woman and still be able to do her job. It was hard to decide whom she disliked most; that common creature, Vera, or Marg, who seemed to think she ruled the roost, or Alice who was young and attractive and had her whole life in front of her. Deep down she suspected it was Alice because she envied her her looks. Stella's blue-eyed, fair-haired prettiness had faded into insignificance, hair and flesh now one-toned, and, she was a stone overweight. And there were now also the unbecoming flushes which mottled up from her neck then suffused her face.

She watched Vera singing. Uninhibited, confident, she was so like the women her husband eventually admitted he preferred. For all she knew Vera might have been one of the ones he was seeing before he left her.

But it was Alice she envied as she watched Jack Winter's son watching her with that look in his eye that men get. The heat rose from her neck and Stella went out to the ladies. "I didn't used to have a temper," she told her reflection in the mirror over the basin as she splashed cold water on her face. "I was always so calm, so capable." But recently there were times when she was overwhelmed with hatred and fury, and vicious thoughts filled her head, making violence not an impossibility. She had even slapped Rebecca the other day, something she had not done even when the children were small.

She went back to work and watched and listened. Boyfriends, men friends, lodgers, and she, Stella Roberts, who was so much better than them, who deserved far more, had nothing.

Vera Langford lived in a high-rise council flat. Unlike her neighbours she was not waiting for a transfer, she loved it. There was no need to draw the curtains, no one could see in but her small lounge and smaller kitchen looked out over the town which sprawled into the distance and, at night, the view was one of which she never tired. Office blocks, their windows randomly lit as cleaners worked or businessmen stayed late, the church of St Mary the Virgin, floodlit from below, the ribbon of lights following the dual carriageway out of the town into the blackness beyond, was what she could see and was far preferable to any rural prettiness.

Leaning against the stainless steel sink she surveyed the twinkling skyline. Better than stars, she thought, because stars hinted at romance and there had been no romance in Vera's life.

She had shared the flat with her second husband and when that marriage ground to a halt she had taken over the tenancy. It was one-bedroomed, unsuitable for the elderly or a family, so it had been easier for the council office to leave her where she was.

She glanced at the cooker clock. Greg would be arriving soon. He had telephoned on Monday, apologising for not ringing sooner but he had been to see his mother and his car had broken down. "It was getting on for midnight, I didn't want to disturb you," he had told her. His wife had gone back to Ireland taking their son with him. Greg was honest enough to admit he would miss him. Vera intended enjoying herself that night. Greg was a soulmate, out for a good time, no strings attached.

37

Her cat, a marmalade she had christened Chivers, wrapped itself around her legs and began to purr. She picked it up and rested her chin on the soft fur. "I'm only good for one thing where men are concerned," she told it, but she wasn't complaining, she had allowed it to happen. Vera, the original 'good time girl' had an image to live up to. Sexy and fun to be with, she was also quick-witted, and men appreciated that. The problem was, the ones who showed any signs of commitment did not interest her and those for whom she felt anything ran a mile as soon as they suspected.

She was ready. Brown leather trousers, stiletto heels and a tangerine blouse. Her hair was loose around her shoulders and her painted nails and lips matched. Chivers' purrs vibrated against her throat.

The doorbell rang, its one-note shrillness startling the cat who jumped out of her arms and fled for safety under the settee.

Greg was a fleshy man with soft pale hair. He wore suits and had a quiet manner of speaking, useful, she supposed in his job as deputy manager of a building society. "A bit like a bank manager," she had said; not that she had ever had a mortgage or managed to save. And he took her to decent places and to the cinema, which she loved.

Tonight was to take her mind off the following morning, when she had a second appointment with a specialist. No one at work knew, except Jack, because Vera Langford was never ill.

"Ready?" Greg asked. "Oh." The telephone was ringing.

"Sod it. I'm for a night out." Vera slammed the door of the flat behind her. They could still hear the ringing as they waited for the lift.

Greg was unusually silent as they sipped their drinks at the bar of one of the town's bigger hotels. "I've been thinking," he finally said.

Vera, high on the bar stool, crossed her legs and tapped the side of her glass with an orange nail as she prepared herself for the brush-off.

"The thing is, I've got some leave to use up. Would you fancy coming on holiday with me?"

"Oh, Greg, I can't. I'm sorry." His disappointment was obvious and she felt obliged to give him an explanation. "I'd like to. It's just, oh hell . . . it's just that I might have to go into hospital." She knew how quickly men backed off at the first sign of illness.

But he smiled at her, which she did not think a wholly appropriate reaction. "Ah," he said softly. "So you're not invincible after all." Vera looked down and studied the vodka in her glass as if it was an alien substance. "Vera?" He lifted her chin with his index finger. "It's not serious, is it?"

"I don't think so. Look, I'm seeing the bloke again tomorrow, perhaps if I push him he might be able to give me some idea of when." Greg noticed the discrepency. *Might* have to go into hospital, she had said before. She was now admitting it was a case of *when*. "I could do with a decent holiday. Can I let you know?"

"Of course. There's no rush." But he was wondering whether it was the thought of a holiday or being with him which most appealed.

James had no secrets from Larry, who seemed to think that under the circumstances, it was a good idea to take Alice out. Larry was also aware that Jack Winter wanted his son to settle down. He was, after all, nearly thirty.

39

That evening, James, perhaps out of nervousness, was a little wild. Like his mother, he was unable to hold his drink, but on occasions, James refused to accept it, or the reasons for it. Around one a.m. he was thrown bodily out of a club and discovered that Larry was no longer with him. He staggered home thinking about the next evening and where he would take Alice. She was certainly pretty and not loud like some of the women, and his father would approve. Yes, Jack would more than approve. Had he not commented often enough that he thought she was wasted at the factory, that she had everything going for her? James had caught his father watching her, thinking himself to be unobserved. Surely he didn't fancy her himself? No, the idea was ludicrous, Jack would never hurt Ruth. Something was wrong at the moment, though. He had walked in unannounced the other evening and interrupted an intense conversation between his parents. They had not resumed it in his presence. He had felt resentful, somehow suspecting that had he been Polly or Simon it would have been continued.

Alice was shaking. Enough was enough. Her anger was still tinged with fear because she thought she had known Keith. His behaviour now was completely out of character. She ran downstairs and knocked on Josie's door.

"Hi, Alice. Goodness, you'd better come in and have a drink. What's up? Keith again?"

"I'm going to call the police, Josie. I can't stand any more, and I'm frightened."

"Calm down. Here." She pulled the ring tab from a can of lager and handed it to Alice along with a glass. "Have you mentioned this to your parents? They might be able to have a word with him. Or his mother."

40

"No. They're worried about me enough as it is."

"I can't see why. Look at you, you're enough to frighten the devil himself." Josie's Welsh lilt was soothing and Alice felt they were becoming good friends. It had been a slow development, neither of them wishing, because of their proximity, to crowd the other. Josie was an enigma. She worked in the office of a firm of solicitors, read serious books and was studying for her legal executive exams yet her clothes were outrageous and if she went out on a Saturday night it was Sunday morning before she returned. Her wardrobe consisted of clashing colours, which she wore in various layers and mostly with heavy boots but where Alice would have looked a mess, with Josie, it worked.

"To my mind," Josie continued, "people who threaten to call the police should do just that. I hope you didn't come down here hoping I'd talk you out of it."

"No." The shaking had stopped. Alice took a deep breath. It was such a relief to be able to talk to someone who was not involved in Winter's Confectionery Company. "I couldn't do it right away, I'd've messed it up. Thanks for the drink, Josie, I'll be off now." She hesitated then said, "Look, if you're not doing anything, why don't you come up on Thursday and I'll make us something to eat?"

"She cooks too!"

"You know what they say about sarcasm." But Alice was smiling. "I'll see you Thursday."

Having started to explain the problem Alice had to start again when she was put through to another officer. "I'm certain it's him," she said, but she was disappointed by the response. No real threat had been made against her person and the officer explained that people used phrases

41

like 'you'll be sorry' or 'you'll pay for this' without actually meaning them. He also pointed out it was a case for British Telecom, not the police. She could get her number changed and make sure it was unlisted, and, if real threats were forthcoming BT would step in.

"But other women where I work have been having these calls too." One each, she reminded herself, and only Vera and Marg.

"It's up to them to make a complaint if they want to, love. I'll tell you what, I'll see if one of the lads can have a word with Mr Wenton when they're in that area, but that's the best I can do. Get on to the telephone people right away, it doesn't take any time these days."

"Thank you," Alice said, and replaced the receiver hoping she had not sounded like some hysterical female afraid to live alone. There was a certain rueful humour in imagining Joan's face if the police did turn up on her doorstep.

Joan, she thought, had to be one of the most miserable people she had ever come across, yet from what Keith had told her she had only been like it since his father had died. Perhaps, years ago, she had been capable of love, or even affection, but now bitterness was all she seemed to experience. What would Joan do if she was on the receiving end of such telephone calls? Probably have a nervous breakdown, Alice thought.

Keith must take after his father. She could not remember Bill Wenton, although the two families had been friends. She was too young when he had died for him to have made any sort of impression on her.

She really ought to eat she thought, but she was restless and jumpy. Lately she wasn't sleeping well and as hard as she tried to think of other things the vague fear lingered.

At least the police knew now and if it was Keith it would stop.

But what if it wasn't Keith? Who else might want to do this to her? What about one of his friends? What about Gary? No, to be fair, he wasn't Keith's friend; he only played football with him. Alice did not like him. He was always boasting about his conquests but saying what he would do to a woman who wasn't faithful. He was just the sort of man who would be only too happy to cause her problems. Not that she had been unfaithful, but to Gary, breaking off an engagement would probably amount to the same thing.

Stop it, she told herself, this isn't doing any good. Not really hungry, she made a couple of slices of cheese on toast and promised herself she would cook a proper meal with plenty of vegetables the next evening she was at home.

The dishes washed, Marg settled down to watch an hour or so of television. Mr Green was studying a fishing magazine. At ten-fifteen he offered to make a final cup of tea. They discussed the weather, one of their main conversational topics. "If the rain keeps off I'm looking forward to Sunday," Marg said.

"And a nice spot of lunch somewhere, save you cooking."

On such occasions Marg always offered to pay her share but Mr Green would not allow it. It had become a ritual, one of the many which had devloped over the years, and at times they were closer than she had been with Monty. But Monty had been all passion; work and drink and bed. Food was no more than fuel to him, eaten at speed to allow him to get on with life. Mr Green was

43

more subtle, able to name trees and plants and he could spend hours at a time on some riverbank under the green umbrella, fishing; not that he ever caught much.

Mr Green glanced at the telephone before he went up to bed. He could not understand anyone doing things like that and he hadn't seen Marg so upset for a long time as when she told him about that nasty call. Still, there had only been the one, and it mightn't have been meant for her at all.

He was always first down in the morning because he liked to wash and shave early to allow Marg the freedom of her own bathroom. They received little post between them and it was not delivered until after they had both left for work so he was surprised, the next day, to see the white envelope in the hall. It was not addressed. He propped it against the biscuit tin where Marg would see it.

"What's this?" she said when she came down wrapped in a salmon silky dressing-gown.

"It was on the mat."

She slit the envelope open with a short, rounded thumbnail. "My God!" she said as she sank into one of the chairs at the kitchen table. Her unmade-up face was pale. She held out the letter. "Go on, read it. It concerns you too."

Despite what he suspected the men under him at work thought, Mr Green considered himself to be totally average. He lived in digs, paid his rent on time, respected his landlady's property and was never late for work. It had taken him years to rise to the level of foreman and he was proud of his position in the timber yard. The next step up meant a collar and tie job. That was not for him.

There had never been any real excitment in his life;

a couple of girls when he was younger, but they hadn't been interested in fishing, all they wanted was a house and babies and saw him as the means of obtaining them. He had come to realise he was probably what they called asexual, feeling no great need for a woman. A simple quiet life was all he wanted and that's what he had. Therefore reading the letter that Marg thrust towards him gave him a jolt.

He kept staring at it, unable to believe that anyone was capable of writing such things. Marg had looked at it once and understood exactly what it meant. Mr Green was not entirely certain some of the things it said were actually possible but he had no experience in that direction.

She was right, it did concern him too, but only in that Marg was accused of performing these acts with him. The vitriol of the letter's contents was aimed at Marg. Not realising that following the telephone call, it was necessary to preserve things like this, that behaving in an ostrich-like manner was not always the answer to something that was less than pleasant, he wanted nothing more than to rid Marg and the house of its contamination.

Marg was watching him, he knew that, but he could not meet her eyes because of those words. She was a formidable woman and he realised she expected some action, that, as the man of the house he should sort it out. He did the only thing he could think of.

"It's vile." Mr Green went over to the sink and held his pipe lighter to one corner of the sheet of paper. When it was no more than ashes he washed them away with water. "There, that's the best thing to do with filth like that."

But Marg was beginning to worry. It seemed to be

escalating and she hated a decent person like Mr Green to be part of it.

"I wouldn't repeat it," Marg said, as Alice spooned coffee into their mugs. "All I'll say is that it accused us of doing unnatural things."

"You must go to the police." Alice placed the mugs on the table. "Look, I had another of those calls last night. I don't know what Keith's up to but it seems our splitting up has changed him. I think he's ill. I've already spoken to the police but I don't think they took me seriously. I mean, letters now, where will it stop?"

"Damn it." Marg lit a cigarette. "I was that upset, I didn't think. Mr Green burned it. Destroyed the evidence, as they say. Anyway, whatever you think, I know your Keith wouldn't write anything like that."

"It was written, not typed?"

"Yes. Bloody great capital letters. I didn't recognise the writing, though."

'Your Keith' Marg had said. He was no longer hers, and he was now a stranger. She saw how irritated Marg must get when Vera constantly alluded to Mr Green in those terms. "Where is Vera?"

"I don't know. She didn't say anything yesterday about not coming in. Come on, it's almost eight."

"She'll be in later," Jack Winter told them when they enquired. "Just a visit to the quack's." He left it at that, it was up to Vera how much she confided in her friends. "You lot can manage for a couple of hours, can't you?"

"Yes." Alice was glad of the extra work to stop her thinking about Keith and the police, and the evening to come.

46

"That's my girl." Jack put an arm around her shoulders and gave her a quick squeeze. She felt the roughness of the Black Watch tartan sleeve against her face and smelled the residue of the cigars he smoked. He had never touched her before. She was surprised, but made no comment.

Later she wondered if it was because James had told him he was taking her out although she had not imagined he would encourage him to fraternise with the staff. But then, she realised, Jack was all right. Her mother had known him since she was a girl, and even Joan Wenton had a good word to say for him.

Seeing how tired Vera was at the end of the evening Greg said he wouldn't stay. "Get yourself an early night. What time's this appointment?"

"Nine-thirty."

"Want me to run you to the hospital?"

"No, thanks, Greg, I've already booked a cab."

He kissed her goodnight and left her in the kitchen filling the kettle. "Make sure you lock up."

"I will." It was a Yale lock. All she had to do was drop the snib and slide the chain across before she went to bed.

"Vera?" As Greg reached the door he saw a piece of paper jammed in the letter box. It had not been visible from outside. He removed it and, immediately spotting the large, black capitals and one or two of the words, stuffed it in his pocket.

"What?" She was behind him with a cup in her hand.

"Nothing. Just let me know how you get on. Give me a ring before you go back to work."

"Okay. 'Night."

47

Her face was pinched but Greg would not dream of saying she looked ill. Vera was not the sort of woman who would take kindly to such a remark.

Only when he was in the car did he unscrew the piece of paper and read it under the interior light. "The bastard," he muttered.

'You're a slut, Vera Langford. A dirty little whore.' Greg read it again. This was the last thing she needed with a specialist's appointment in the morning. He did not know because he had not asked and Vera had not told him, what was wrong, but he could see she was worried. He knew Vera's reputation: there had been men, many men if rumour was to be believed, but so what? She had never done him any harm nor did he think she was seeing anyone else at the same time. They got on well, they both knew how to enjoy themselves. Perhaps someone was jealous and wanted to come between them. Perhaps, as there was no envelope, he was meant to see the note.

When he got home he tore it up and put it in the bin.

"Look at me," Alice said to her reflection in the mirror in the heavy, old-fashioned wardrobe in her bedroom. This time she was nervous with anticipation and wondering what on earth she and James would find to talk about. She slipped her best dress over her head. It hung in soft, tan folds, the lining cool against her skin, and emphasised her slimness. She chose drop ear-rings, three wooden balls to each, separated by thin, silver rods. They swung as she moved her head. Flattish, brown shoes and a handbag that was once Liz's matched close enough. She had blow-dried her hair. It needed a trim, the tapered fringe was resting on her eyebrows.

But she managed to apply liner and mascara without smudging it.

James was punctual. He smiled and took her arm and opened the passenger door of the car for her. She was reassured when she suspected his own hands were not entirely steady either. Only when he said he knew a nice restaurant and they were on their way did she wonder why she had not mentioned to anyone that James had asked her out. Protection, maybe, in case it was just the once, but also protection from Vera who was quite capable of embarrassing her in front of Jack.

"I think we should tackle her." Marg nodded in the direction of the table where Stella Roberts sat alone, sipping her tea with both hands around her mug as if she was cold. Her back was to them.

"But what can we say?" Alice chewed a thumbnail. The three of them had remained in the canteen during the lunch hour deciding what action they could take. "And she's bound to deny it anyway." Marg had said her caller might have been male or female and now Alice was wondering if it was possibly a woman. Only on one recent occasion had she been entirely sure it was Keith.

"No, I think we should leave it." They looked at Vera with surprise. She was not one to hold back, but she had just told them she was to have a hysterectomy which must have upset her. "I think we should mention it to Jack."

"Why?" Marg flicked a disobedient, peroxide curl into place.

"Because if it *is* someone here, it's best sorted out by him. I mean, imagine what the atmosphere'd be like if we go around making accusations, especially if we're wrong. Stella's bad enough as it is. And there's always

49

the possibility it's someone else, someone who's got access to our records, maybe."

"You could be right. And don't forget that bloke on the mixing machines, the one that fancied you. You remember, Vera, he was a real nuisance until you slugged him one."

"That was a year ago. Besides, why would he want to get at you and Alice?"

"OK, I'll have a word with Jack." It was taken for granted Marg would be their spokeswoman. "And while I think about it, what's making you so smug?"

"Smug? Am I?" Alice grinned but did not elucidate.

That evening Alice was slicing salad vegetables when there was a knock on her door. It reminded her that she had not yet done anything about changing the telephone number. It was too early for Josie and she was not expecting anyone else. Nervously she went to answer it, opening it only a few inches. "Mum! Come in."

Liz, elegantly dressed in an olive skirt cut on the bias and a cream blouse and jacket, followed her daughter into the kitchen. Alice looked strained, not all at her usual vivacious self. And why had she been afraid to answer the door? "I was just passing," she said.

"Well, you'd better have a glass of wine. I'll have one too while I finish this." Alice smiled at her mother. Liz's dark hair and complexion and the gold hoops in her ears were somehow paradoxical against her clothes, giving an impression of half tamed wildness. Alice was proud of her mother's looks.

Liz found two glasses and a bottle of white in the fridge. "Someone special?" She indicated the table, set for two.

"Josie downstairs." Alice opened a cupboard and took out a packet of pasta. "Mum, I went out with James Winter last night."

Because Alice was draining some olives she did not see the involuntary start which caused Liz to spill some wine. "I see," she finally said. "Did you go somewhere nice?" She had known Jack and Ruth for many years. Most people knew, or knew of them, reminded of their existence by the ever-present cloying smell of chocolate which hung over the town unless there was a breeze.

"Um, a restaurant. A sort of bistro, I didn't know it existed. He's nice, not at all what I expected, and he's a bit shy."

"Are you seeing him again?"

"Yes. On Saturday." She was puzzled, Liz's tone seemed unnecessarily sharp. Maybe she thought that two and a half months was too soon to be seeing someone else after breaking off her engagement.

"Look at the time, I'd better go," Liz said. She kissed her daughter on the cheek. "Dad's taken the car in for a service and I'm supposed to be picking him up in mine as we're going over to the Lawsons'."

"Have a good time."

"You, too."

Alice put the salad on the table and sat down to finish her wine. Last night had been nothing like her evenings with Keith. Once James had known she had not already eaten they went straight to the restaurant. Both food and wine were excellent, but she guessed James could afford it. They had talked about Winter's Confectionery Company and the conversation had flowed from there. Afterwards Alice realised she had done a lot of the talking and that she had learned little about James except that he

51

liked reading. He was, she soon realised, also aware of the end of her relationship with Keith. He must have been interested, she thought, to take the trouble of finding out if there was someone else.

"Dad told me," James had informed her.

At the end of the evening they had both become more relaxed. James had dropped her outside the house which contained her flat having, she noticed, drunk very little. When he had got out to open the car door it had crossed her mind he might have expected to be invited in. "Oh," she'd said with a small laugh when he shook her hand and thanked her for an enjoyable evening. "I enjoyed it too."

The sort of lives the Winters led probably made them adept at the social graces but she did not think James was just being polite. She hoped he liked her as much as she was beginning to like him . . .

Another knock on the door brought Alice out of her reverie. This time it was Josie.

Joan Wenton had not been over to visit the Powells for a long time because she felt uncomfortable that their respective offspring were no longer together. However, she had made up her mind to telephone Liz to see if she could talk some sense into her daughter. It took two evenings of calling before she found Liz at home.

"I've been meaning to ring *you*," Liz said, "but what with work and one thing and another . . ." the sentence trailed off. There had been a time when Joan had been a real nuisance. Just after her husband had died and for almost two years after, Joan would turn up at inopportune moments, usually when they were about to eat, and pour out her troubles. Naturally, at first, Liz had been more than pleased to help her through a bad time, but she and Derek did not seem to have a minute to themselves, and Joan had made no effort get on with her life. Now, Liz felt vaguely ashamed for not having contacted her. "Anyway, how about, ouch! Sorry about that." Liz was grinning. Derek, on his way to the kitchen, had whacked her across the bottom with a rolled-up newspaper. Joan would wrinkle her nose in digust if she told her. "Why don't you come over tonight? We're not doing anything."

"No, not tonight, I've got a few bits to see to." Joan wanted to set her hair. Next to Liz she always felt frumpy. It was the only time she was aware of her own appearance.

"Tomorrow then?"

"Yes. Fine." Joan replaced the receiver. Keith was upstairs, she could hear the water running.

When he came down, showered and shaved, he said not to lock up. "I might not be back until late."

"But, I . . ."

"You what?"

"Nothing, dear." He was a good-looking boy, fit and strong, and he seemed, at last, to be coming to terms with his disappointment. "Before you go, could you fetch me my pills, the ones I take for my dizzy spells?" She sank into an armchair in the old-fashioned, uncompromising living-room. The furniture was dark and heavy, the armchairs firm and upright with wooden arms and a clock ticked away the boring minutes Keith spent in that room. Joan thought comfort led to idleness.

Keith sighed and went to the kitchen. He could not understand why she persisted in these dramatics for he had long since stopped giving in to them. No doubt she expected him to offer to stay in and sit with her. There

53

was nothing medically wrong, he was convinced of that, but she refused to take an interest in anything outside the house and himself.

Tonight he was meeting a couple of mates from work. They were going to have a drink then go to one of the clubs. If he was to stand any chance of meeting someone else – and he could see Alice's point now – it would not be standing at the bar of the football club. Keith was saddened anew at the finality of it and he did not really want anyone else.

"I kept it. Look." Alice showed them the letter that had been pushed under the main door downstairs some time late on Thursday night or early that morning. It was in a plain, white envelope, marked *'Alice'* and consisted of only one line. *'You should learn how to treat men properly, Alice,'* was all it said.

"Well you have to admit, you can't really construe that as a threat." Marg studied it as though she may have missed something. "It's the same writing, though. We'd better show Jack."

"No." Alice snatched it back. If Jack discussed her with James, then he would surely mention the note and she did not want the relationship to start off with any complications, nor for James to think she mixed with the sort of people capable of such actions. Marg had, however, already had a quiet word with Jack, who had promised to make some discreet inquiries. But Jack had not seemed terribly interested; his mind had been elsewhere during their brief conversation and Marg knew something far more important was occupying his thoughts.

"Touchy this morning, Alice, aren't we? A bit different from yesterday." Marg patted her hair knowingly.

"I'm sorry. I'm tired." And she was. Sleep did not come easily lately and she was beginning to think that Vera was right, that there was some sort of vendetta against them.

Vera was oblivious as she scrutinised her red-tipped fingers. The surgeon had explained that there was a very short waiting list at the moment, that she was one of the lucky ones. She was uncertain whether that was fortunate or not.

"We've all been assuming it was Keith," Marg continued. "Well, he has got a motive, losing Alice like that, and he knows how close we are: he might want to get at all of us. I mean, think about it: suppose he believes we put her up to it, breaking off the engagement? But what puzzles me is that we've all known him for ages and I just can't see that it's the sort of thing he'd do. I still say it has to be someone here."

"You're not still thinking of Stella are you?" Alice, too, when she really thought about it, found it difficult to imagine Keith could be so cruel. Stella Roberts was an extremely difficult woman to like. Each, in turn, had tried to draw her in, to include her in their conversations but she insisted upon remaining aloof, as if she was looking down her nose at them. They had discussed the possibility of the telephone calls and letters being her handiwork, except it was unlikely Stella would be able to disguise her rather high-pitched, nasal voice enough to convince them it was a man.

"Maybe. Or what about the lovely Phyllis? She's got ready access to our addresses and telephone numbers."

"We all know that, Marg, she's got everyone's details. But why pick on us?"

Marg shrugged. "I don't know, Alice, but have you

55

got any better ideas?" Surely, now she'd mentioned it, Jack would have a word with Phyllis and, as caring as he was about his staff, would have no hesitation in sacking her if she were the culprit.

There was no further chance to voice their opinions because it was time to start work.

"Stop idling and get on with it," Jack snapped, taking them by surprise. He was not usually so abrupt.

Jack? Alice wondered. He seemed to be under some sort of pressure lately and she was sure he was giving her strange looks. Was it possible that now he knew her relationship with Keith was over he was trying to torment her in some way? No, why should he? And why pick on the others?

"I've got a nice piece of belly pork tonight," Marg said as Mr Green hung his maroon anorak on the hook in the hall and meticulously straightened the sleeves. Monty would have slung his jacket over the back of a chair and left it for her to put away.

"Lovely. You know I like a nice bit of belly pork." He followed her to the kitchen and sat at the table with the evening paper as Marg, in stretch trousers tucked into fur-lined boots, moved from worktop to sink, from sink to cooker in the same way as she had almost every night for the past thirty years. Once she caught his eye. Had he been watching her? For a split second Mr Green became a suspect, but only because it was all so mysterious and worrying that she knew she was not thinking rationally. Accepted, it was Mr Green who handed her the letter, or, rather, propped it against the biscuit tin, but what possible reason would he have for upsetting any of them? Besides, she told herself sternly, he did not know the surnames or addresses of her friends.

She joined him at the kitchen table with a mug of tea while the vegetables cooked and could not prevent herself from taking a surreptitious glance at the crossword he liked to complete each day. The block capitals which now filled most of the blank squares were sloping to the right and far more angular than those contained in any of the notes.

"Are you all right?" Mr Green asked. "You seem a bit on edge."

"Yes, I'm fine." Marg smiled. Occasionally he called her by her name although initially it had been Mrs Finch until she said it was a bit too formal for two people who slept under the same roof, albeit in separate rooms. He, in turn, had reciprocated but Marg could not bring herself to call him Hilary. "Monty and Hilary," she often said to herself. "Two men have shared this house with me and neither of them has had a nice ordinary name like Bill or Jim or Harry." Now they got along very nicely by calling each other Mr Green and Mrs Finch, respectively, in public, and nothing at all at home.

Chapter Four

Phyllis Greenslade had worked for Winter's Confectionery Company for twenty-one years, starting as a tea-girl-cum-dogsbody. She had learned shorthand and typing at evening classes, although the former was a dying art thanks to audio machines. Now and again Jack would call her in and dictate a letter, but her speed was much slower through lack of practice, and she guessed Jack only did it to remind himself of the old days. She had surprised herself at being able to master the word processor which replaced her electronic typewriter, which, in turn, had replaced the high-backed Olivetti Jack had dumped somewhere or other and which was probably almost an antique.

Phyllis was single and lived alone in a dreary flat which had once been bright and modern. Once her chance of marriage and a future had disappeared, she had stopped bothering about her surroundings, not caring that the paintwork needed doing and the carpet was wearing thin.

It was as if Cyril had taken the juices of life with him when he left her: from being soft-skinned and rounded, Phyllis had lost weight, becoming haggard and looking older than her years. Her hair had turned prematurely grey and she wore it in an uncompromising

French pleat and her skin sagged where once had been healthy flesh.

She had eventually learned to live with the humiliation, even the humiliation of knowing the women on the factory floor knew her background. Some months before, a temp who had come in to help until a full-time assistant could be found, had overheard a conversation between herself and Jack which referred to the past. The temp, with nothing to lose because she was leaving the following day, had gleefully repeated the contents of this conversation to the women when they were on the bus that evening. Phyllis had her own car so had not been aware of it until the following Monday morning when the pitying glances she had received had left her in no doubt as to what had happened.

Her feelings about the women were ambiguous; one minute wishing she was one of them, the next pleased that there was no one to whom she owed explanations or apologies, or even courtesies. Men did not come into her calculations; she hated them all, with no exceptions. Even Jack, she admitted to herself, Jack who had displayed neither shock nor sympathy but simply listened and said he would keep the job open for her whatever she decided to do.

What an absolute fool those women must take her for. What an absolute fool she had been. Cyril, with his looks and generosity, was nearly twenty years her senior. He had wined her and dined her and sent her flowers and always acted the gentleman whilst Phyllis was unable to appreciate her own, gradual seduction. Certain he would marry her she had allowed him to share her bed and was naive enough to think she would not become pregnant.

Needless to say the 'perfect gentleman' had shown his

true colours when she told had him, and had called her a conniving bitch.

"I thought you'd marry me," she had sobbed, doubly distressed at her predicament.

"Marry you?" Cyril had laughed in her face. "I don't imagine my wife'll take too kindly to that idea."

Phyllis had been too speechless to beg or plead, at least for some assistance, and later this was the only thing for which she was grateful; she had not demeaned herself further in his eyes.

And all that humiliation had been for nothing: the painful visit to tell her parents the news, the discussion with Jack about how she stood at the factory and the final humiliation when the temp had spitefully given away her secret. Phyllis had miscarried quite early in the pregnancy, perhaps because of her mental state or maybe because she had stopped looking after herself. She always rather hoped it was one or the other, rather than a natural phenomenon because, had the child survived, she was sure she would have hated it.

Until that temp had come along she had almost successfully managed to put the past behind her, to pretend it had happened to someone else, not the efficient, hard-working Phyllis Greenslade she had become. Her well-kept secret had re-emerged after eighteen years and only then because Jack had called her in to tell her that his daughter, Polly, had just learned she was expecting his first grandchild and that he wanted to tell her first, in private, so as not to upset her in front of the others.

"It's a long time ago now," she had said. "I'm no child to be taken in by a married man again. And as for the baby, my life has been happier without it." The subject was only briefly touched upon but enough was said for the girl, who, passing the door, had stopped to listen for a few seconds and to put two and two together.

Phyllis sometimes had occasion to get out one or other of the women's files. She would stare at their details with envy. The single were all young and unencumbered, with their lives ahead of them. The rest were married, with families, although one or two were divorced and Marjorie Finch was widowed. It seemed not to stop her enjoying life: Phyllis knew she lived with a man she claimed to be her lodger, and Marg was ten years older than herself.

They tried, she supposed, to make an effort, asking her out for a drink but she had always refused, so they no longer bothered. She had shut herself off from humanity so successfully that she was unable to see that there would have been no criticism, implied or otherwise, and that her past was a matter of indifference to the women.

She was going through some invoices when Jack rang her on the internal phone and asked her to come into his office.

Jack had forgotten his conversation with Marg. Knowing she was inclined to dramatise, he had taken what she told him with a pinch of salt. His concern at the moment was two-fold: the future of his business, and that of his son. James had shrugged off the idea of coming in full-time, although Jack was not certain what he could find for him to do, and now was the least appropriate time to be thinking of taking on more staff. "Phyllis," he said, "I'd like you to ring Peter Cousins and arrange an appointment. Try to get him to come here. Failing that, I'll meet him for lunch at the Green Dragon, but I want to speak to him on my terms."

He had decided to let Phyllis make the call to his

rival; he did not want Cousins to have any idea what the discussion was going to be about and be questioned over the telephone; Jack was afraid he might give too much away prematurely. He had already gone over his tactics with Ruth who would, he knew, go along with whatever he thought best. Nevertheless, he would not dream of making major decisions without consulting her.

Phyllis wrote down the details and turned to leave. Through the glass panels she saw Alice Powell glance up at the movement. The Alice Powells of this world don't know how lucky they are until it's too late, she thought, as she made her way back to her own office.

Over the noise of the ancient vacuum cleaner Alice did not, at first, hear the tap on the door. Kicking the switch to off, she ran a hand through her hair and thought it was probably the electricity man wanting to read the meter.

"Oh, no."

"Alice, please don't shut the door." Keith pressed a palm against it to prevent her doing so. "Please, just listen to me." He looked haggard and Alice thought he might be on the verge of a breakdown.

"What do you want?"

"The police came to see me."

"Yes. I sent them. I did warn you."

"It isn't me. Wait. Believe me, I wouldn't do those things."

She paused. He was so familiar, his face, his body, the smell of him, and he was wearing the blue shirt with the dropped sleeves she had bought for him.

"I know I've made a nuisance of myself because I wanted you back, but I haven't rung anyone else and I certainly wouldn't threaten you. Oh, Alice . . ."

62

She believed him, she could see the sincerity in his face. And then he ruined it. Holding her by the upper arms he pulled her to him and kissed her. She jerked back and struck him across the face.

"I'm sorry." Keith knew he was finally defeated. He turned and walked away.

Alice recognised his quiet dignity and felt ashamed, but her anger was partly with herself for having responded, if only briefly. But there was no time for reflection, James was due in fifteen minutes.

They listened to the car radio as they drove out into the country, a distraction Alice was glad of until she felt calmer. Settling back into the comfortable seat she was lulled by James's confident handling of the car.

"A walk?" he suggested.

They parked in a lay-by, ahead of which was sign for a footpath which was reached by means of a stile. James held her hand to help her over it but, to her disappointment, released it immediately. Underfoot the ground was soft and damp, last autumn's leaves sodden and decaying, their earthy richness rising pleasantly as their feet disturbed them.

James was thoughtful. Once he turned to her as if to speak, then changed his mind. When they reached a boggy patch they had to turn back because neither of them had suitable footwear. "Something to eat now?" he asked.

"Yes." Alice looked at her watch: it was already after two, too late for a pub meal.

"There's a village about a mile further on, we'll try there."

The village was neither quaint nor picturesque. It was a working village, serving a farming community. Mud trailed down the road, deposited by tractor wheels, and there was the smell of dung from the corner of a field. There were no souvenir shops, no olde worlde tea shops, but there was, however, a local store which served several purposes. Outside were two rusted pumps, one for petrol the other for diesel for the farm machinery. Inside were shelves holding a selection of basic grocery and household goods and at the back, through an archway were some formica-topped tables, several men with mugs of tea and and an aroma of fried food.

"Well, places like these are often the best," Alice said optimistically. She was wrong. The coffee tasted peculiar, it was probably mixed with chicory, and the bacon sandwich was fatty. Keith would have laughed with her but she made no comment; she did not yet know James's moods.

James was not thinking about the food, he was watching the other customers casting sly glances at Alice. In tight, blue jeans and a sweatshirt her slender curves were clearly visible. The men were ogling her and he was angry, yet he could not understand why he should be.

Alice, noticing the faint pinkness of his cheekbones, tried to make conversation, and, found herself wanting to touch him, but not now, not there in front of those people.

They drove back as the sky darkened and a squally shower hit the windscreen. There was a five o'clock showing of a film Alice wanted to see. "We might as well," James said, "there's not much else to do." But she was unable to enjoy it because of his lack of enthusiasm before and during the film. Something was troubling him but she did not feel she could ask what it was.

"Do you like curry?" he asked.

"Yes." She grinned. "There's nothing I won't eat."

"Good."

James's mood changed. Throughout the meal he was charming and entertaining and made her laugh. "I always eat so much in Indian restaurants, I feel I may never want another meal," he said, when they'd finished.

"It was very good."

"Ready? Come on, I'll drop you home."

"I, uh, okay . . ."

He saw the surprise and disappointment in Alice's face. "Didn't I say? I promised to go to my parents' tonight, they're having some sort of do."

Alice's smile was tight. He confused her. One minute it seemed he really liked her, the next as if he wanted to get rid of her.

When he pulled up in one of the few vacant spaces in her street and leant across the seat she imagined he was about to kiss her. Instead he opened the car door for her to get out.

So he's just not rushing me, Alice decided later as she picked up a book. She had not planned to spend the last few hours of a Saturday night reading. She tried to convince herself she was glad, that it was a chance to relax after a busy day. But it was not doing much for her ego.

Once she found it was impossible to concentrate, that she was rereading the same paragaph, she let the book slide to the floor. James was an enigma, more so since he seemed reluctant to tell her about himself. Finally, after some gentle teasing on Alice's part, he had said that his job wasn't worth discussing, that he was filling in time until he took over his father's business, that he helped out a market research company by analysing their findings. She must be mistaken, but she was sure Jack had once said James had no interest in confectionery. Still, he was often popping in, perhaps she was confusing him with Simon. It seemed, too, that James had no hobbies, or none that he wished to discuss.

Well you can't have it both ways, girl, she told herself when she was in bed. You moaned enough that Keith had too many hobbies which took priority over your life. But surely a man in his late twenties must have developed some interests? And then the telephone rang. This time the threat was unmistakable.

"You're drunk, Vera." Greg just managed to keep the accusation light enough not to offend.

"And so am I," she retorted loudly, before collapsing in a giggling fit. Greg grabbed her arm as she tottered precariously on three-inch heels.

They had started the evening at the Chigago Bar where they had had several cocktails, or Vera had. Greg had stuck to a gin and tonic because he had, quite rightly, assessed the way things were going. He had booked a table at a Greek restaurant but by the time they were due there Vera had decided she was no longer hungry. It worried him, this constant dieting, especially as she was already so thin, and she still had not told him why she was going into hospital. Each time he raised the subject she neatly avoided giving him an answer. Sensing her mood and deciding he had no choice but to go along with it, he ordered a taxi to take them to a pub she had named where a jazz band was performing. Finally, but with difficulty, he persuaded her it was time to go home. Outside the lift on her floor, he took the doorkey from her hand because she was unable to get it into the lock.

66

"Let's get you to bed."

Vera, hand on hip, leered. "There's nothing I like more than an eager man."

"Come off it, you're in no state . . . Vera!" Her arms were around his neck as she swayed, unbalancing them both. Greg lugged her towards the bedroom door where she lurched the three necessary steps to reach the bed and collapsed on it, giggling. He waited until her eyes started to close then removed her shoes, turned her on her side and covered her as best he could with the half of the duvet she was not lying on.

Vera enjoyed a drink, so did he, but he had never seen her in this state before. Standing in the living-room he was undecided what to do. What if she was sick and choked in her sleep? "Damn and blast the woman," he said to the empty room before trying to get comfortable on the settee which was too short for him. He hoped he might manage a couple of hours sleep himself.

Joan Wenton studied herself in the speckled glass of the cheval mirror in her bedroom. Grey hair neatly set, navy skirt, white blouse, navy cardigan and shoes. "You can't go wrong with navy," she told her reflection.

She was more hurt than pleased that Keith was delighted to hear she was going out, but she explained it was her duty to keep in touch with old friends.

The evening air was damp. Joan took a scarf from her pocket and tied it over her hair to protect her efforts with curlers and dryer. In a grey raincoat she set off for the Powells' house. The hiss of hydraulic brakes meant a bus was waiting at the junction at the end of the road but it wasn't worth hurrying to the stop to catch it as it was only a ten minute walk.

Joan couldn't understand Liz. If she'd had a daughter she would never have allowed her to live in a flat by herself, as Alice was doing – especially when she worked in the same town. There was no need for it and it was an unnecessary expense. Still, that was Liz's business.

A stiff breeze stirred the bare branches of the trees. Joan retied her headscarf. It was a funny time of night, half dark, half daylight, people indoors having their tea or watching the TV, and those men that had no sense of family, in the pub having a couple of drinks before going home. Bill would never have done that. He liked to watch the kiddies having their bath and he knew her rules about meal times. His reward was to go to the local at ten or just after, that way it was certain he couldn't have too much.

Joan had decided that once she'd got this thing sorted out with Liz and Derek, she would have a quiet word with Alice. It was all very well Keith going out with his mates in the evenings now, but she had to make sure it didn't continue. Alice, she felt, would be too slack, would allow Keith to take liberties. Of course, as they would be living with her she could put her foot down if necessary. It would be cosy, the three of them in the evenings, then later, after a respectable period, a baby.

She *must* succeed. That Jackie Pearce had been sniffing around Keith, and from what Joan had heard she was out drinking with her pals almost every night. There was no way she wanted her son becoming involved with a girl like that.

The evenings were drawing out now but it would be nicer when the clocks went forward. Joan glanced into front rooms as she plodded along the road. Balloons were tied to a gatepost; inside the house a children's party was still in progress. She tutted. They looked no more than five or six. Her two would have been in bed long before.

Derek opened the door and Joan grimaced. What could she smell? Garlic, surely? I'd like to know how anyone can eat the stuff, she thought, as she followed him into the house.

Although the living-room was the same size as hers, there the similarity ended. Liz's three-piece suite was soft and comfortable, the lighting subdued and the mock coals of the gas fire flickered soothingly. Joan prefered a good, strong overhead light, that way you would not damage your eyes.

"Gin and bitter lemon?" Derek held up the bottle of Gordon's.

"Just what I could do with, too." Liz smiled from the doorway. "How are you, Joan? It's good to see you again."

Joan attempted a martyred smile in return as she took in Liz's black velvet ski-pants and soft blue sweater; items of clothing that would never see the inside of her own wardrobe. Her hair was shiny and dark; the gold hoops swung. I bet she uses a rinse, Joan thought uncharitably.

Derek tactfully enquired after her eldest son and placed a bowl of the cheese biscuits she liked onto the table beside her. He winked at his wife as they waited to see how long it would take Joan to get to the point. It did not take long.

"I don't wish to seem interfering," she said. Liz bit her lip in exactly the same way Alice did when she was trying not to laugh. "But the thing is, I'm really worried about Keith. He's taken it very badly, you know. I never

69

did get to the bottom of what their little disagreement was about, but surely you can talk some sense into Alice? I can understand she might have needed some space – I believe that's what they call it these days, but it's three months now."

"Alice is a woman, Joan. She makes her own decisions. And it was more than a disagreement, surely you realise that? To be honest, she wanted more from life than football and darts."

Joan was affronted at this criticism of her son, but Keith had admitted as much himself.

"Besides, she's seeing someone else now," Liz added.

"Is she?" asked a surprised Derek, not aware of this development until now.

"Already? She didn't waste much time," Joan responded, frostily.

Liz did not point out that a few minutes ago Joan had made three months seem an eternity.

"Anyone I know?" Joan pursued.

"Yes." There was the slightest hesitation. "James. James Winter."

Joan clamped her mouth shut. Even her Keith was no match for the Winter family. Then she remembered something. "Is that wise? I mean . . ."

Liz shook her head almost imperceptibly. It was enough of a warning to Joan who had always been afraid of the other woman's confidence and outspoken manner. If she said anything out of place now there would be no chance of Keith getting Alice back.

"It's such a waste," Derek commented when Joan had left.

"What is?"

"She is. If only she'd take a bit of trouble with her

70

appearance or find something to do with herself she'd be so much happier. When I see the two of you together it's impossible to believe you're the same age."

The flattery was satisfying but Liz's hands were shaking as she poured them a final drink.

James sat on his bed, fully clothed. It was almost two a.m. but sleep was impossible. He could not get Alice out of his mind. He liked her, more than liked her, and she did not make him feel the way the others had done. He knew he ought to get married at some point; his family expected it, and he had chosen Alice because he believed she would be so grateful for all he could offer her that she would not mind about the other thing . . . And she would be an asset, looking as she did, so unlike the ubiquitous, brittle blondes his father's friends and his own contemporaries seemed to pick. But what he was experiencing was confusing and therefore frightening.

He had lied to her, he was not seeing his parents, but he could not think of another valid excuse at the time. He had needed to get away, to think, because he did not know what to do or how to act.

Larry had laughed at him, called him a fool and reminded him women were only there for one thing: men's convenience. And Larry had tried to get him drunk but for once James had been strong and Larry had failed.

James lay back, hands clasped behind his head as he looked forward to seeing Alice again.

As soon as the caller hung up, Alice depressed the connecting bar of the telephone and, once she had the dialling tone, arranged to have her number changed. She should have done it sooner. For the first time in her life she felt real fear as she tried to recall exactly what had been said. The threats were of a sexual nature, explicit, crude and revolting. She had been unable to detect an accent or the sex of the caller because the words had so shocked her, made her feel sick. "I'm twenty-four," she said aloud to break the awful silence in the room, "I cannot go running home to my parents." Which was what she felt like doing.

Tomorrow she would buy another lock for her door. It was Sunday but the big DIY store was open. Her father would fix it for her.

Dawn was framing the curtains before she finally slept.

Detritus from Saturday night was blowing down the back alley and into Marg's small yard when she opened the gate to put the dustbin out ready for Monday morning. The dustmen came early and she sometimes forgot by the time Sunday night came. She picked up some chip papers and a polystyrene burger carton and threw them into the bin. There was a Sunday morning quiet, back curtains still drawn in some of her neighbours' houses.

The washing was on the line and the tea and toast dishes had been washed up. Only a small breakfast Mr Green had said, they didn't want to spoil their lunch.

Satisfied that everything was in order, they were ready to go. Because it was Sunday, Mr Green wore a tweed jacket over his sleeveless jumper instead of his anorak. He also wore a tie.

Marg thought she had better dress for the occasion too and chose a red skirt with box pleats, a white, frilly blouse and a red and white cardigan. It might be cold on the coast so she stuck to her fur-lined, suede boots.

Mr Green went out to warm up the engine while Marg locked up. She placed her raincoat on the back seat of the blue Volkswagon Beetle and levered herself into the passenger seat.

Mr Green drove sedately out of town and took the coastal road. The journey took just over an hour. Once there, they found a car-park and Mr Green placed a handful of coins in the 'pay-and-display' machine although no one else seemed to have bothered. "You can't be too careful," he said when Marg told him he was wasting his time and that traffic wardens only came out in the summer.

The resort comprised a small, modern shopping precinct, locked up out of business hours, an old-fashioned high street and the sea front with its uninspiring view of grey, choppy water as far as the horizon, where it merged with an equally grey sky. Along this stretch were souvenir shops, amusement arcades and fast-food outlets, but most of the premises were boarded up and would remain so until Easter.

Despite the stiff breeze they walked the whole length of the promenade and back again, Marg's hair hardly moving because she had lacquered it well. "Does you good, a drop of the old ozone," Mr Green said, sniffing the air.

Marg raised a darkened eyebrow. All she could smell was frying onions from one of the few burger stalls remaining open.

Mr Green was disappointed that there was no proper café or restaurant open for Sunday lunch. "It'll have to be a pub then," Marg said quickly enough, because she was ready for a gin and orange. They found one which overlooked the sea and took their drinks to a table in the window. The menu was chalked on a blackboard on the wall. Mr Green pulled out his glasses to read it. The place was filling up and they had to wait for their food. Marg took the opportunity to buy another drink: a second half of bitter shandy and, as she was paying, a large gin for herself.

"Nothing like a nice piece of haddock," Mr Green said when the meal arrived. "I always make a point of having fish when I'm by the sea. Stands to reason, it's got to be fresh."

Marg snorted. "I don't see any fishing boats, besides, there's no harbour here. That battered haddock came from the same freezer centre as my Chicken Kiev, you mark my words."

Undeterred, Mr Green still insisted he could tell the difference.

Warm and full and comfortable, it seemed a shame to have to leave. They had a stroll around the town, looking in shop windows and when the first drops of rain hit the pavement they hurried back to the car and decided to call it a day.

When they got home there was another white envelope on the mat.

James was unable to see Alice on Sunday because Simon was down from university for the weekend and they were all going to Polly's for a family lunch. Alice had been expecting this because Jack had mentioned it earlier in the week and she, too, was in a similar situation.

As her mother would be setting up the table in the sewing room, Alice decided to make an effort and wear her new pinafore, even if her brother turned up in jeans.

She hoped to have a moment to talk to Liz. Alice was finding that having made one change – in finishing her relationship with Keith -- she was now re-evaluating other aspects of her life.

I've become too settled at the factory, she thought as she made the half-hour walk across town. It had been a stop-gap, a way of earning money after she left school until something suitable turned up. But Jack had made it too easy, because her wage was more than that offered in many of the advertisements in the local paper, and it was fun working there. And there had been Keith. It had seemed pointless to change until after the wedding. I'm better than this, she told herself but felt disloyal to Jack for doing so.

Noise and warmth and cooking smells greeted her when Liz opened the door. Mark, Nicola and baby Damien had already arrived. The television was on and Mark and her father were glued to the screen as the big sporting event of the afternoon was being discussed in depth beforehand, as if it could make any difference to the result. Damien was screeching for attention and being ignored because Nicola was reading the paper and seemed immune to the noise. On seeing Alice he tottered over to her and grabbed her around her legs. She picked him up and kissed him, glad his hands weren't sticky on her new clothes.

"Hi," Mark said, without taking his eyes off the screen.

"Hello, love." Derek managed to tear himself away for a quick grin. Nicola smiled warmly then carried on reading. She was always quiet and calm, a protection, Alice guessed, from the incessant demands of a hyper-active toddler.

Liz inclined her head towards the kitchen door and

Alice followed, her thinking how small the house seemed with them all in it. As a child, with the luxury of two downstairs rooms, it had seemed large.

"It took me most of the morning to clear the back room out, but it needed doing. The junk we've collected." Liz was slightly flushed from the heat from the oven, but otherwise unruffled. "I like the outfit."

"It's new."

"Ah, yes, to go with the new man. How's it going?"

"Fine. We went out for the day yesterday." Liz's back was turned. "Mum, I've been thinking."

Liz stopped stirring the gravy and looked at Alice. Her daughter's face, even when serious, was still pretty.

"It sounds daft, but I feel I'm wasting my life."

"In what way?" Liz asked.

Alice shrugged. "I go to work, go out, all the usual things, but I keep feeling there should be more to it than that. I'm not achieving anything. Does that make sense?"

"Yes. I felt the same once."

"But not now?"

"No. I got married young and had you two quite quickly. Only when I was in my thirties did I wish I'd had some sort of career. It was too late then, for me anyway. Life had sort of taken over. Strange, really, I'm quite contented now. Must be old age."

"Not you." Liz was forty-five but looked younger. It was hard to imagine her parents getting old.

"Have you got any plans?"

"No, not yet. I thought I'd like to go to college, get some sort of qualification. I didn't do too badly at school, I should be all right. The problem is I've got so lazy I can't even decide what I want to do."

"Look, if it's money we —"

"No. Absolutely not. I was thinking of evening classes anyway." Alice smiled. She had been half-expecting the offer but the whole idea was to do something for herself.

Liz grinned back. The stubborn tilt of Alice's chin showed her it would be useless to argue. "All right, but you'll have our backing whatever you decide. Now go and tell them it's ready and to turn off that damned television before I throw something through it."

After lunch, Alice helped with the washing-up and stayed chatting to Liz in the kitchen. Mark and Derek were esconced in front of the TV again and Nicola was putting Damien down for a nap. At four o'clock Alice left.

The weather looked unsettled. A bank of cloud hung low in the sky with darker clouds in the distance. Alice walked quickly and tried to think what she wanted to do with her life. Tonight there was only the television or a book to look forward to; she had seen both the films she wanted to see at the cinema. The trouble was she no longer had any friends of her own age and she had no interests, nothing to occupy her spare time.

At the entrance to the park gates she hesitated, then went in. A walk would kill an hour or so. She began to realise she was a late developer intellectually and that now she really felt ready to start learning. But what? Learning for its own sake was not what she wanted, she needed to be able to put it to use later. "And I need to met more people." She blushed when a man who was showing his small son how to sail his boat on the pond turned to stare at her. She had spoken aloud.

Alice walked on past the bandstand which was no

77

longer used and came to the open area where the council football pitches were. Keith played there sometimes, possibly even that morning. By the time she reached the far gates she was chilly because she only had a baggy, belted raincoat over the pinafore. It made her appear more waiflike than she actually was.

The clouds became more threatening, so she turned back. In the wide main street she stopped to look at the incongruous summer clothes in the shop windows. The gaudy colours and geometric designs were not for Alice; pale, simple things suited her best. A reflection made her look up. Her eyes were narrow as she turned around.

Keith held out both hands, palms forward, as if to ward off an attack, verbal or possibly, after their last encounter, physical. "I just happened to see you. I was on my way to the club to put some new lights in for them. It's a favour, funds are low as always. The van's there," he pointed, and continued so as not to give her a chance to speak. "I'll give you a lift, it's starting to rain."

It was, and Alice was cold.

"Just a lift."

"All right," Alice said. They walked to the van and got in, the tool boxes, rubbish and paperwork a familiar sight.

"Can we be friends?" Keith concentrated on the rear view mirror as he waited to pull out. "I won't pester you any more, Alice, I give you my word. I never meant to upset you. And it's daft going on like this. I'm doing my best to start afresh."

"Oh?" She hoped her tone implied lack of interest but she was curious. Impossible not to be when she had spent four years of her life with him.

"I've started going out with the lads from work and I even took Jackie Pearce for a curry."

"Jackie?" Alice stared at him. Was the gleam in his eyes gloating?

"Yes. Apparently she's fancied me for ages, not that I'd noticed."

Alice was not in any doubt that their relationship was over but it gave her a jolt to think that Jackie had had her eyes on Keith all that time and that, despite his actions, he was not so heartbroken it had prevented him from taking someone else out. Ego, she realised, was a fragile thing.

"How about you?"

"I'm seeing James Winter actually," she was glad to be able to say.

Keith whistled. "I bet he doesn't take you down the football club."

Alice laughed and when Keith joined in she knew it would be all right, that if, in future, she saw him, alone or with someone else, there would be no embarrassment and no anger. "Oh, I nearly forgot, can you drop me here? I need another lock for my door."

"What sort? A bolt?"

"Yes."

"No need then. I've got one in the back of the van. It's not new but it's a good one. Want me to put it on for you?"

"Would you?"

"It won't take a minute, and I've got time to fix the lights before the club opens at seven."

Keith went up to the flat with her, put the bolt on with practical efficiency then left, refusing the offer of a cup of tea.

Alice closed the door behind him, feeling safer and pleased that they seemed to have resolved their differences.

She had not noticed the car parked in the street, the driver watching through the wing mirror.

Chapter Five

James had not particularly enjoyed being at Polly's. Even amongst his own family he felt an outsider and he did not have his mother's ability to let things wash over him.

"Your sister went to a lot of trouble over that meal," Jack said as they drove back. "And you hardly opened your mouth."

"Leave it." Ruth gently placed a hand on Jack's sleeve. James needed careful handling. He was the one who always seemed most troubled. There was pain in his eyes but she did not know what caused it. Jack told her she saw problems where there were none, but he was wrong, and all she wanted was for her son to live a happy, contented life, as she did herself.

James walked away from the car without saying a word. Later, realising he had been rude to his mother, he returned. Jack had gone to the golf club to have a drink with a business associate and Ruth was listening to music as she read. The lounge was long and high ceilinged and glass doors led out to the garden, illuminated now only by the lights spilling out from the house, the shrubs a bluish green in their glow.

"Are you all right, James?"

"Yes, I'm fine. Drink?" Ruth shook her head. James poured a small measure of brandy into a glass and sat on the beige sofa placed at right angles to the one where his mother sat. More and more Alice was occupying his thoughts. She was no longer engaged to Keith, he told himself. Over and over he repeated it in his head. She was no longer seeing Keith.

Ruth rested her book across the arm of the sofa. "James, can't you talk to me? Please tell me what the matter is."

James sighed. He did not really know; sometimes it was difficult to think straight. "I've been seeing someone. A girl."

Ruth waited. Maybe, at long last, James had found someone who could make him whole again, who would take him out of himself, who would even marry him. She often became tired of coping with his moods, the long silences when he was deep in thought or when he seemed not to hear if he was spoken to.

She listened without interruption as he tried to explain his feelings. "I know you were both trying to help, when you invited girls over to dinner, but they were too, I don't know, demanding I suppose."

Ruth thought she understood. The girls were from families who socialised. They were confident, outspoken, and expected men to be equally or more so. James appeared that way but with him it was an act, learned from copying his father. Initially, it had been that way with her, too, and, she suspected for many people, until the act became natural, part of one's personality. It had not happened with her son.

Maybe a quiet, gentle person was what he needed. Opposites did not always attract. Whoever it was, she would welcome her and make her feel part of the family as long as James was happy.

"Is she pretty?" It didn't matter, Ruth simply wanted to keep him talking, to get him to say what was really on his mind.

"Oh, yes. Very. And slim, petite really." James sat down, hands clasped between his knees.

"She sounds lovely. I'd like to meet her. Where did you meet her by the way?"

"I didn't. Not exactly. She works for Dad."

Ruth felt her body tense. She swept her hair back in an effort to seem casual. "Do I know her?"

"You've seen her. She was at the Christmas party. Her name's Alice. Alice Powell. Mum, what is it?"

Ruth was rigid in the chair, her face pale. She gave a small laugh. "Nothing, I'm all right."

But her dreams for James's happiness were shattered and she had no idea what to do. Discussing it with Jack was impossible, telling James utterly impossible. She needed time to think, to find a way of solving the problem with as little pain as possible. How James would cope with it was beyond her imagination.

"I really can't believe it." Vera's face registered near panic. "I thought it would be ages, but they want me to go in next week."

"That quickly?" Marg was amazed. She had had to wait several months for a simple D & C. "Look on the bright side, the sooner you're in, the sooner it's all over."

They were grateful for the mid-morning break as the coach had been late that morning, made later still because Stella Roberts had not been at the stop and the driver had had to wait for her when he saw, in his side mirror, her figure hurrying down the road. The scornful look she had given the women as she made her way, breathless, down the aisle, had caused a few raised eyebrows.

They were at their usual table, the one nearest the urn where, if they were quick, they had time to make a second cup. Marg smoked her one cigarette. Vera, Alice noticed, had already left three lipstick-stained butts in the tin ashtray.

They took no notice of Stella when she entered the canteen until she bypassed the urn and stood, arms by her side, red-faced, a plump bundle of fury. "I know you don't like me," she hissed, "but it's gone far enough. Which of you bitches sent me this?" Her voice was rising, half in anger, half in an attempt not to cry. She slapped a small, white sheet of paper on the scarred and ringed table. The three women stared at it without moving. There was no need to read it, they recognised the large, black capital letters.

It was Marg who picked it up. *'No wonder your husband left you, you frigid old cow,'* it said. She put it down again. It was hurtful and hateful. Stella was not a particularly pleasant woman but she had been through a bad time and circumstances may have made her that way. And, if what she said was true, she had lost everything she once had. No one, not even Stella, deserved this.

Marg silently passed the letter to Vera. Alice read it over her shoulder.

Marg was thoughtful. "Come on, Stella, sit down."

"Sit down? With you?"

"Sit down." Marg's tone was firm enough for her words to be obeyed. "When did you receive this?"

"This morning. That's why I was late. I wasn't going to come in at all at first." She did not add that she had

84

been close to ringing up to say she would not be coming in any more.

"You aren't the first."

"What?" Stella's mouth dropped open.

"Me, and Alice, we've also had nasty letters." She paused. "And to be honest, Stella, it crossed our minds that you might be behind it."

"Me? You thought it was me?" Her voice had risen and the scarlet flush was creeping up her face. "Why would you possibly think it was me?" But this was said more quietly, as if she was addressing herself.

"Be realistic. After all, you thought it was us." It was the first time Vera had spoken throughout the interaction.

Stella bowed her head but was unable to disguise the flush which had now suffused her whole face, and which was the cause of so much embarrassment.

"Enough's enough," Marg stated. "It's time we did something positive. I'm in favour of going to the police. Who's with me? I made sure I kept the second note, have you still got yours, Alice?"

"Yes. It's here in my bag. But they're not overtly threatening, and they told me they couldn't do much unless they were."

"But the phone calls were. We'll go, we must. Tonight after work. All agreed?"

They were, but Alice wondered what sort of an idiot they would think her for not taking their advice and having her number changed immediately.

Marg noticed that when they went back to work, Stella was about two or three feet nearer than where she normally stood, and her face had returned to its natural colour. There was a clank as the prongs of a forklift truck hit the concrete floor and a whirr as the conveyor belt behind them started up again. A maintenance man asked them to move out of the way so he could put his stepladder up to replace one of the fluorescent tubes which had been buzzing and flickering irritatingly prior to extinguishing itself forever.

Half-pound boxes of plain chocolates with hard centres were the next items to be placed in cartons ready for distribution. Their packaging was stark but refined – expensive-looking, unlike the selections for the resort trade which had a bright and breezy picture of the pier or gardens appropriate to the town and a message declaring it was a present from that area. Jack used a good designer which had made Winter's confectionery stand out from that of other manufacturers. It was surprising no one had tried to steal his ideas before.

Jack's meeting with Peter Cousins took place that lunchtime but very little had been achieved at the initial talks. Jack had put forward his proposals, only one of which might be acceptable but Cousins was not a man to jump into any deal at the first opportunity. He had immediately turned down Jack's offer to buy him out. Having consulted the bank and his accountant, he was in a position to do so but only with the aid of a loan. Jack was honest enough to accept that he had realised this proposition would meet with a negative response. His second one, timed to come after the first, and very cleverly thought out, was the more realistic, and the one with which he hoped to succeed, although he allowed Cousins to believe it was the other way around.

"All right," Jack had said, "I can understand you don't want to lose what you've got. Neither do I. And

I'll admit it, I've been slowly losing trade because of your cheap copies of our designs. I've made a success of my business by doing things myself, not by imitating others, and I'm sure that's not what you intended." Not much, he thought, as he smiled with all the charm he could muster. "So, I've spoken to the design company I use, and they are confident they can come up with a different packaging for your products – but just as good as ours. And as a favour to me, they'll charge you less than the going rate. What do you say to that?"

"It's something to think about," Cousins told him. Not that much thought was needed. He had ridden on the back of Winter's, and now was probably the perfect time to make his own mark. However, unlike Jack, he was not aware that quality packaging was not enough. His goods were inferior and his firm would never reach the sales figures Jack's had achieved. Jack lit a cigar. He could wait. He knew he had him.

"Alice, got a minute?" Josie was waiting with her flat door open. "Oh, shove those on the floor," she said as Alice looked around for somewhere to sit. The room was as untidy as ever: textbooks, newspapers and dishes were scattered around but seemed to cause their owner no embarrassment. "Tea, coffee or wine?"

"Wine, I think."

"Surpermarket claret, but it's not bad. That solicitor I was telling you about, the one I ran into in the County Court, he's asked me out."

"He hasn't?" Alice smiled. Josie had been talking about him for weeks.

"Took him long enough." She pushed her hair back; the sides were plaited with thin ribbons. "Actually, I don't think he had much choice, I couldn't have made it clearer."

"Honestly!" Alice realised with that one word, she sounded exactly like her mother.

"I'm meeting him on Wednesday. What about you, are you still seeing whatsisname? The Candy King?" Josie listened as Alice told her the extent of their relationship. "He's not married, is he?"

"No. Why?"

"Because I've been through it. Seeing someone once or twice a week, and never late, and hardly at all at weekends."

Alice frowned. The pattern fitted. "No, of course he isn't." Her laugh was one of relief. "Don't forget, I work for his father, I'd've known." Jack often spoke of his family. But she was sure Jack did not know James was taking her out and for unidentifiable reasons of her own she had not mentioned it to anyone at the factory.

"Good. It is not a pleasant experience. And I deceived myself more than anyone else. I believed the lies because I wanted to believe them. Still, that's history. Want another drink?"

"Mm, please." She held out the smudged glass. "We've been to the police."

"About those calls? About time too. Not that they were overhelpful the last time."

"But there're the letters too, and now another woman at work's started getting them."

"Are you sure it isn't someone at the factory? Surely that's the logical conclusion?"

"We had our suspicions about one person, but they were unfounded. Only Jack and Phyllis in personnel have access to our records." But Jack, as an employer, treated them almost like family. Phyllis though, what sort of a woman was she? They knew of her past, at least, Alice corrected herself, they had heard gossip about her past. Like Stella, she was aloof, perhaps thought herself a cut above them because she worked in the office, but was she disturbed enough to go to such lengths? It was something to be discussed with the others before mentioning it to Jack. "At least it's officially on the police files now," she added. "I'd better go, Josie. Thanks for the drink."

In her own flat Alice automatically kicked on the switch of the fire then realised, for the first time that year, its heat was not necessary. Plugging in the kettle she tried to decide what she wanted to eat but her thoughts kept reverting to what had gone on at the police station. If the sergeant on duty behind the desk had been surprised at seeing four women bearing down upon him, his face did not register it. They were asked to wait before eventually being taken to an interview room.

The outcome was not very promising. The interviewing officer also seemed to believe it was more than likely someone at their place of employment, someone who bore them, as a group, a grudge. It was too coincidental to be anything else especially as no other residents of the town had made any similar complaints recently. Alice's face had been red when she had related what she could recall of the sexually explicit words she had heard before she had finally decided to change her number. And Phyllis, she thought, now had that new number.

Some inquiries would be made but the four women were told that the police did not have the resources to keep their homes under constant surveillance on the off-chance of catching the person responsible for delivering the letters. They were given some advice

89

about security and warned not to go out alone after dark, which did nothing to add to their peace of mind.

Alice felt she needed to talk about it. It was time to tell her mother.

"What about Keith?" was Liz's immediate reaction.

"No, I'm certain now it's not him. And why the others?"

"Joan then. She's desperate for you and Keith to get back together," Liz continued. "She might think she can scare you and you'll go running back to him for protection. I know, before you say anything, it's the last thing you're likely to do. Don't think I don't know what a stubborn young creature you are."

"Joan?" The idea had not crossed Alice's mind, but she knew Keith's mother was probably capable of such a thing. There was still the question of where she would have got the addresses, though, and telephone numbers. The names would be familiar because Alice had often mentioned her friends, and besides, now she thought of it, Stella Roberts had not started at the firm until after she and Keith had split up. "No. She might do it to me, but not the others."

Liz chewed a thumbnail. "I don't know what to say, love. But for God's sake, be careful, and take notice of what the police told you. I can't help worrying about you, old as you are."

Alice reassured her mother that there was no chance of anyone getting into her flat. The main entrance door was secure and Josie, a light sleeper, would hear if someone tried to break in. When she had hung up she realised what a dirty feeling it was, this suspicion of everyone she knew.

*   *   *

90

The week was drawing to a close. Marg had had another consultation with Jack, who began to take her seriously when she told him the four of them had been to the police. He promised to have a tactful word with Phyllis, not a task he relished, but he realised there were rumours flying around and the sooner they were squashed, the better.

Under the lipstick and blusher Vera was gaunt. Monday, and her admission to hospital, were drawing nearer.

Alice watched the women from other areas, trying to assess whether it might be one of them. No, it came back to the same things. Why? And how would they know where they lived?

She had seen James twice during the week. The first time they had had another meal, the second, he had taken her to the theatre to see a musical, which the critics had slated, but she had enjoyed.

Friday afternoon came and Jack had still not had a chance to speak to Phyllis. A machine operator had injured his hand and had to be taken to the casualty department of the nearest hospital as the wound was too deep for the sick-bay nurse to attend to, and Jack himself was stalking around as if he was on edge. No one knew he was still waiting for a reply from Peter Cousins. "I don't bloody well believe it," he stormed when a man in a white boiler-suit and head gear came up to speak to him. A batch of mixture for the soft centres had been ruined because the ingredients programme for the computer had been wrongly entered. The filling, which should have been pale pink, was more like blood than strawberry cream. "What a way to end the week." He ran a hand through his hair which was already ruffled.

Few had escaped his wrath that day and as the hours passed without the telephone call for which he was waiting, his anxiety increased. Had Peter Cousins simply accepted a free meal, listened to what he had to say, then gone away laughing? And, to be fair to his staff, he really ought to speak to Phyllis. Now, maybe, before she went home? It was not as if she had to be on the coach. Yes, now. He might as well get it over with rather than have it hanging over his head until Monday.

Phyllis was pale but calm when he broached the matter as delicately as he was able. But there were few ways you could ask a member of staff if they had been sending poisonous pen letters and making obscene telephone calls.

Phyllis denied the implied accusations firmly and politely, hiding her inner turmoil adequately from a man who had enough other problems that her own were less easily discernible.

"I hope I haven't caused offence, Phyllis, but you see I had to ask. No one else has access to those files."

"It's quite all right. I understand." She did not say that Jack had access too. In fact she did not say anything else at all. She simply went back to her office for her coat and, standing up, wrote a letter of resignation which she sealed in an envelope, addressed it to Jack, marking it private and confidential, and left it propped against her word processor. This was the final humiliation.

Because she wanted to repay James for the times he had taken her out, Alice invited him to her flat for a meal. As they were going out on Saturday afternoon it was easier to keep the food simple so there would be no fiddling around when they got back. She purchased smoked mackerel paté from the delicatessen and rang her mother to ask her to get a couple of steaks. There would be salad, and fruit and cheese to follow.

She was beginning to feel slightly more relaxed, as since her telephone number had been changed, and was ex-directory, there had been no more obscene calls. It had also, however, occurred to her, when giving her new number to those who needed it – family; friends; Jack, for his files – that James had never given her his home telephone number, nor asked her for hers. Josie's words came back to her. Was he, after all, married? She forced the disquieting thought away.

The flat was clean and tidy, the salad prepared and the steaks in a marinade when James arrived. Alice knew she looked good in a gathered skirt with embroidered hem, tan boots and a scooped neck jumper of fine wool. It was mild, so all she needed over the top was her linen jacket. Out in the street she saw that something was wrong. James's skin was grey and there was sweat on his top lip. "I think I'm coming down with something," he said, when she enquired.

But James knew it wasn't that. It was Larry. Larry wanted to meet Alice – was, in fact, being quite persistent about it. And that must never happen. James hoped he was strong enough to prevent it.

It was a disappointing day. They drove down to the coast and parked near the dunes, but a walk along the beach did nothing to alleviate James's pallor. He spoke only in answer to questions.

"Shall we go back now?" Alice asked him. His silence was unnerving but his expression was forlorn. She was tempted to take his hand, to make him look at her and tell her what was wrong but a growing anger stopped her. She had moulded herself to Keith's way of life and was not

93

about to make the same mistake. Nor was she prepared to cope with moods which were none of her doing but simply inflicted upon her without explanation.

They were in Alice's street before James spoke. "I have a friend, Larry."

"Oh, yes?" Alice assumed this friend was ill or in trouble. His next words confused her:

"We're very close."

She waited.

"He worries me at times."

"Worries you?"

"Yes."

"How?"

"It's difficult to explain. He says he wants to meet you."

"I'd like that." It was the first time he had offered to include her in the life that was his before they met.

"I've got to go." He leant over and threw open the passenger door. "I'm sorry."

Left standing on the pavement she watched the car disappearing at a speed too fast for the road.

A mixture of anger and compassion made her restless. The food no longer seemed appetising but at least it would keep. Alice looked ahead to another Saturday night alone. Another reminder of Josie's words. So it would be a bath, a couple of glasses of the wine that was to have gone with the meal, a few more chapters of her book, then bed.

Noises from traffic and people still in the street at midnight prevented Alice sleeping. She turned on the bedside light and studied the brochure from the adult education centre which she had not looked at properly. There were several courses which interested her. She circled these in red ink leaving the final decision until the morning when she would be less tired. Gradually the sounds from outside decreased and she fell into a deep sleep.

Late on Monday afternoon Jack Winter came down the stairs from his office with a grin on his face. "I thought you'd like to know, I've just rung the hospital and Vera's fine. She's come round from the anaesthetic and comfortable, as they say. Greg's there with her at the moment but she can have other visitors as from tomorrow."

Greg, Marg thought, was a different kettle of fish from most of the men Vera became involved with. He was standing by her when she most needed it. Vera, she guessed, would be taking it harder than she was letting on; this proof that she was no longer a young girl. "Thanks, Jack," she said. "We were just wondering how things were going."

"Alice?" Alice looked up and was puzzled by the expression on Jack's face. There was concern in his eyes which seemed to be more for her than for Vera. Her position was still unclear. Did Jack know she was seeing his son and perhaps disapprove? No, he wasn't like that. She wanted to ask him but was unable to find the words to enable her to do so. Jack had always been good to her and she suspected he put himself out for her more than for the others but she put this down to being the youngest in the group and because he knew her parents. However, Jack was not his usual cheerful self lately; she hoped it really was none of her doing.

Jack returned to his office. Still unsure as to her motives, he reread Phyllis's letter of resignation. It stated that under the circumstances she felt she could no longer remain at Winter's Confectionery Company. What circumstances? he thought. What did she mean by that? Did she know more than she had been prepared to admit or were his questions simply a catalyst? Her letter also stated that her obligatory week's notice was covered by a week's holiday owing to her, and requested that her holiday pay was sent on to her, as she would not be back. Jack sighed. Perhaps it was for the best. Phyllis's work had become sloppy recently.

Alice and Marg decided to go and see Vera together the following evening. It was left to Marg to buy a suitably suggestive card, one which Vera would appreciate, from the newsagent's on her way home but Alice would chose a gift in her lunch hour. She had organised a collection in the packing section.

Alice had received no note, no message of any kind from James on the Monday night, so she had persuaded Josie to go out for a drink. If he called around on Tuesday she would be at the hospital, at least, early on.

Stella had taken to sitting tentatively at the end of their table during their breaks. Marg had watched with amusement from beneath her peroxide curls. Finally, during the Tuesday afternoon tea break she said, "For heaven's sake, woman, move your bum a bit closer!"

Stella felt the hot flush creeping up as she took the seat next to Alice and wondered if it was possible she could get to like these women.

"Well, well, if it isn't the Winter's Confectionery drinking league. I'm surprised Miss Singapore let you both in at once with Greg here."

"I'm just going," he said, kissing the top of Vera's head.

"Miss Singapore?" Marg took the chair Greg had vacated and Alice sat on the end of the bed.

"Sister. She's Chinese or something."

"How do you feel?" Alice enquired.

"Like shit to be honest, Alice. And they won't even let me have a ciggie. And there isn't a minute's peace. They want to do something to you every five minutes. Still," she grinned, the lipstick a gash in the ashen face but more like the old Vera, "the junior doctors are all right."

"And Greg?" Marg tried not to appear too inquisitive.

"He's been great. He's keeping an eye on the flat and feeding Chivers for me. Here, have you seen this lot?" She indicated to a basket of fruit and two vases of flowers. "Jack sent them in. Must've cost a fortune."

"He can afford it," Marg said cynically.

They only stayed half an hour because, despite Vera's efforts to convince them otherwise, they saw she was tired.

"I'll be home at the weekend," she said. "For God's sake come and visit me. I've got to take it easy for a while and I'll go out of my mind with boredom."

"Where's the lav, love?" Marg asked on their way out.

"Down the corridor on the right," the Chinese sister replied, affronted at the familiarity of Marg's words.

For the first time in her life Phyllis Greenslade had made a spontaneous gesture. Even though she cried herself to sleep each night over the weekend, she did not regret resigning. She had never fitted in at work, except with Jack, and on those occasions James came and chatted to her, she had never been sure if he was mocking her.

She knew the women had tried to be friendly, but they were not her sort. It was doubtful, with all the bitterness she harboured, that she could form a close relationship with anyone.

It was time for a change and Jack's veiled accusation had prompted her to make it, if a little sooner than she had anticipated.

The whole business with the telephone calls and letters was obscene and, after what she had personally experienced, she had a very good idea how those women felt. But there was something on her conscience, something she could not admit to because she was not sure if she was right. It was better, she decided, to say nothing than to leave herself open to further humiliation.

On Monday she would set about finding another job. One thing was certain, she knew Jack well enough to realise she would get a good reference.

Joan Wenton was becoming obsessed with the idea of seeing Keith and Alice back together. Joan knew she had failed in trying to get Liz and Derek involved, but perhaps there was another way . . .

Keith had mentioned that he was now dating Jackie Pearce and that had shaken her. Jackie was no Alice; she was harder, an extremely determined young woman and quite capable of taking Keith away from her. But Joan had never seen beyond Alice's prettiness and therefore was unable to credit her with the qualities she possessed.

Her thoughts went back over the years to two decades ago. Such a long time had passed it was hard to recall the rumours exactly, but if she was right Joan knew she could use them to her advantage. No it wasn't rumours, she corrected herself, it was something Liz had said. And instinctively Joan knew that Jack Winter was unaware of what was going on between James and Alice. Well, I'll be doing no more than my duty in letting him know, she thought.

Joan had known the Winters for many years, since the days when Jack started to make his mark – when his father had begun to suffer from senile dementia but managed to conceal it long enough for Winter's Confectionery Company to almost go under. Jack's hard work had saved the firm and the jobs of those who worked for him. His father was dead now, but his mother still lived. She occupied a modern bungalow, built for her by her son, and led an active life. Far more active than Joan's.

Joan had been at school with Jack's youngest sister and had gone to tea with her on several occasions. Eventually she had had to ask Eileen back to her own house, ashamed of the 'two up, two down' poverty of their lives; the stone sink in the kitchen with its single cold tap, and nothing but bread and dripping for tea followed by stale cake left over from the weekend. Eileen had not batted an eyelid, she had to give her that, and claimed to enjoy the dripping as she dug her knife to the bottom of the bowl in search of the dark, rich jelly.

I'll speak to Jack as one parent to another, Joan decided, as she dialled the number. It was Ruth who answered the telephone.

"Joan Wenton? Yes. Just a moment, I'll get him."

"Hello?" Jack remembered her from his youth. She had been a plain, dumpy child then, and prone to snivelling. He could never understand the friendship between Eileen and Joan. On the few occasions he

99

had met her as a woman, he had thought she had not altered much.

"I can't see what the problem is," he told her, after she had dropped her bombshell. "Of course we knew," he bluffed. His voice was steady but his mind was in turmoil. "Alice's private life is her own affair, as is that of my son. Goodbye." He replaced the receiver and took several deep breaths.

At least I didn't swear, he thought. How any woman could demean herself to tittle tattle in the hope of causing trouble in such a way, was beyond him, but he had not let the side down, he had not been disloyal to his family. But did Joan know what had happened all those years ago? Is that why she rang? She had implied nothing, though. No, impossible. No one knew, only Liz and himself. He needed to speak to James urgently. It was several minutes before he was composed enough to deal with the situation.

Marg sighed with relief as she eased her feet out of the fur-lined boots. As an antidote to wearing the things at work she favoured feminine mules at home; wedge-heeled, pale pink and swansdown pompoms on the velveteen band across the toes.

Mr Green would be away for the weekend as he was participating in a course fishing competition and this evening he would be preparing his equipment. It was a change to have only herself to think about.

On Saturday morning the weather was balmy, a prelude to spring proper. Marg decided she would visit Vera after she had had her hair done. Taking no chances she slipped a headscarf and a plastic rain hat into the jacket of her red blazer.

At eleven-thirty she rang the bell to Vera's flat. Damn, she thought. It was Greg who spoke into the entry phone. She had hoped to catch Vera alone. Vera let her in. Marg noticed her friend was still pale but looked better, she also noticed the protective way in which Greg's hand rested on Vera's shoulder as he stood behind her chair.

"What's new?" Vera lit a cigarette.

"Not a lot. And it seems as if those letters et cetera have stopped. Whoever it was must have known we'd been to the police."

"The police?" Greg sat down and leant forward. "What's all this about Vera?"

"Marg and Alice were getting weird phone calls, then letters. We thought it was someone at work. Seems like we were right. I had one too but as it was only the one it wasn't worth mentioning."

"How do you know?"

Vera frowned at what she believed to be Greg's stupidity. "Because I answered the phone, of course."

"I see. That wasn't what I meant. Look, I didn't say anything before, but the same night you told me about seeing the specialist there was a note pushed through the letterbox."

"Then you should have given it to me. I won't have people interfering with my mail, Greg, no matter what it contains."

"Hold on, let me explain. It wasn't in an envelope and it wasn't addressed to you. Also, it was anonymous and when I saw what was written on it I thought someone was trying to come between us. I wanted to protect you, Vera, that's all. You were low enough as it was."

"I don't need protecting. Just tell me what it said."

Marg lit a cigarette of her own, vaguely uneasy

101

at being caught up in what might develop into an argument.

"All right. It accused you of being a whore. Satisfied?"

Vera studied Greg's face through a cloud of smoke. His concern, she saw, was genuine and his intentions well meant. And he was far more easily shocked than herself. She grinned. "Well they're wrong. I've never done it for money."

"Vera!" But some of the anxiety had gone from Greg's eyes.

Marg coughed to remind them she was there then sipped her coffee. She had had to bite her tongue to prevent herself making an acerbic comment along the lines of Vera making a fortune if she had done so.

When she left she knew that whatever bond Vera and Greg had formed, it was strong enough to withstand more than they had been through together already. It was a cheering thought.

Peter Cousins had deliberately taken his time in informing Jack of his decision although he had made it almost instantaneously. He telephoned the factory on Tuesday morning and suggested they meet at six for a drink.

Jack was no fool. Impatient to hear his answer he still made Cousins wait whilst he ostensibly checked his diary. He had tried to hide his anxiety both from Ruth and from his staff but he had been on the receiving end of some strange glances recently and knew he had not totally succeeded. Tonight, hopefully, his worries would become a thing of the past.

"I didn't want to lose it all," he admitted to Ruth later

that evening. "After all my efforts when Dad became ill, all those years getting the business back on its feet I was so scared it was going to turn out for nothing."

"Cousins has agreed to your terms?" Ruth knew how hard he had tried to keep it from her and to keep his temper which was on a short fuse although his anger was soon forgotten. The tiredness was etched in his face; in the web of lines around his eyes and the dullness of his skin.

"So he says. He's agreed to give our packaging designer a go."

"People are fools, Jack. Surely they could tell the difference."

"Only once it was too late. Cousins' chocolate is inferior but you don't know that until you've eaten it. I bet you automatically reach for things in the supermarket because you recognise, without really looking, what it is you want, even when the shelves are changed around."

Now she knew about Cousins, Ruth reflected that she had been wrong about the cause of her husband's tense mood this last few days. She'd assumed he knew James was seeing Alice, and worried about the possible consequences. But Jack's shock on hearing it from Joan the other night made it clear it was news to him.

"How long have you been seeing her?" Jack Winter asked his son, casually. On telling Ruth about his telephone conversation with Joan, he had been shocked to learn that Ruth was already au fait with what was going on, and, more so that she hadn't chosen to tell him.

"Why? What's it to you?"

"Careful, son, when you're in my house you behave with a bit of respect."

103

James ran a hand through his hair, a gesture character-istic of his father. "Sorry. I didn't say anything in case it made things awkward for Alice."

"In what way awkward?"

"At work, I suppose. If people knew she'd get an awful lot of teasing about going out with the boss's son."

"And you thought I'd tell the other women?" James did not realise that a bit of embarrassment about going out with the boss's son would be the least of Alice's worries if the relationship got serious. He sat down, tired and defeated.

"No, I didn't think that. But why the inquisition?"

Jack shook his head. He could not answer that. Not yet. Hopefully, not ever. "Forget it, James. I've been under a lot of strain recently." And you're not helping, he added silently, wishing his son would find a job and not go around pretending he worked in some sort of consultancy capacity. It put him and Ruth in an embarrassing position. They refused to lie for James but at the same time they avoided discussions on the subject so as not to make *him* out to be a liar. "Just don't hurt her," he said. "Alice is a lovely girl, I don't want to see her upset again." And that was as much as he felt able to say about the subject. Alice was level headed, he must rely on her good sense. Surely, like the women before her she would soon tire of James.

The only consolation was that apparently no one else was aware of their relationship. What frightened him was how far it had progressed.

James was surprised at his father's reaction but the problem of Larry was becoming more pressing. Larry was becoming a nuisance, insisting that he meet Alice and he had told him what he had seen the other day and although

James did not want to listen, he had known it to be true. He was desperate to get closer to Alice but had no idea how to go about it. And then, in frustration, on Sunday night he had picked up a girl. She was scrawny, wearing cheap clothes and perfume. Her skirt was too short and she stank of sweat and alcohol. Her enlarged pupils made James think she was on drugs. She had invited both him and Larry to a party. James offered to drive them but said he would not stay himself. On the way he realised he should have used the gents in the pub. He had pulled in and relieved himself behind someone's garage and then Larry had got into the back of the car and started tearing at the girl's clothing. What shocked James was that he had done nothing to prevent it happening. He had viewed the scene as if from a distance, partly with revulsion, partly with enjoyment. He supposed it wasn't strictly rape, the girl had hardly struggled and seemed not to care what was going on, but it was the next best thing. Larry said it was a punishment, that someone had to pay for what he had seen.

"Get out!" James had shouted. "Get out and leave me alone." The girl half fell out of the car and stumbled away up the road oblivious of her ripped tights and smudged make-up.

When he started the engine Larry had also gone. James drove home quickly, sweat running down his back. There was, he knew, one way to get rid of Larry but there was a price to pay and he did not want to have to go through all that again.

Forgetting the conversation with Jack and trying to forget Sunday night, James knew he could no longer postpone contacting Alice. He felt sure he had lost her but had been afraid to hear it for certain. The last time he had seen her was when they had gone to the coast and he had let her down over the meal.

On Wednesday evening he went around to her flat. The worst that could happen was that she would refuse to speak to him. His relief was immense when she opened the door and smiled. "I'm in the middle of the ironing," she said, indicating the board set up in the middle of the lounge. She switched off the radio and asked if he wanted anything to drink.

"No, I'm fine, thanks. Alice, about the meal, I'm really sorry, I was ill. Even so, I shouldn't have let you down like that."

"It's all right. Forget it." In her working clothes, her face washed and shiny Alice looked young and innocent and James saw what his father meant about hurting her. As yet he had no idea of her stubborness and inner strength.

Alice continued ironing and told him she was trying to decide between two courses: one at the local college on business management, the other from a magazine advertisement Josie had shown her. She did not mention that the second one was full-time in case James told Jack and he started looking for a replacement before she was ready to leave. James did not look particularly pleased at the news but there was to be no more pandering, no more making it easy, she had done too much of that with Keith.

"Would you like to go out somewhere?" James asked.

"Not tonight," she said pleasantly, "I've got this lot to do."

"Would you like me to leave?"

Alice relented. "No. Are you hungry? If you can wait until I've finished this I could make us something to eat."

It was, in a way, a test. If he was prepared to sit and watch her ironing he must think something of her.

"Lovely."

The conversation moved on to work and Vera's progress and Stella Roberts. Alice had already mentioned that she was a difficult woman to get on with. "But she seems to be mellowing. Mind you, it's probably because of the things that have been happening."

"What things?"

Alice rested the iron on its end. She might as well tell him. He might already know if Jack had said something. But as she outlined the harassment she and the other woman had suffered she saw James's hands were clenched. She was amazed at the extent of his reaction. It seemed that he could barely contain his rage.

"The bastard!" he exclaimed, hotly.

"Well, it seems to be over now," Alice concluded. She took the iron out to the kitchen and as she folded up the board she decided she had been rash in inviting James to stay for supper. But there were enough bits and pieces to make a sauce to go with some pasta.

They did not move over to the settee when they finished eating but remained at the table, talking. Alice explained that she had promised to visit Vera the following night. James said he would take her out on Friday. "If you're free," he added. "Oh, and don't make any plans for the weekend after."

"Why?" Alice queried.

"It's a surprise."

Alice smiled. He obviously had not lost interest. In that case she would put forward her own invitation. Until now she had not been sure how it would sound. Taking a man to meet your mother suggested a permanence neither of them was ready for. But Liz had suggested it last time they had spoken on the phone. "Your father says why don't you bring him over for Sunday lunch?" was how it had been phrased. For some reason her mother did not seem too keen on the idea of James Winter. Alice dismissed the thought: perhaps she was being oversensitive because she was still unsure of her own feelings.

James responded to the invitation enthusiastically, saying he would be delighted to meet her parents. He then got up to leave. In the doorway he turned, tilted her chin with his forefinger and kissed her. Alice kissed him back. His flesh tingled but his brain was filled with images of Larry and the girl. He pulled away, he did not want to contaminate Alice with his vile thoughts. "Goodnight," he said. "I'll pick you up on Friday."

At last, Alice thought as she cleared the table. It was their first kiss, she had enjoyed it, but James had taken so long to make a move that she had begun to wonder if there was something wrong with her or if he simply did not find her physically attractive. They were getting somewhere and there was the weekend to look forward to.

Chapter Six

Vera was alone when Alice arrived at her flat. Dressed in leggings and a sloppy jumper, her face free from make-up and the roots of her hair showing darkly, Alice suddenly saw how Vera could almost be the mother of someone her own age rather than the exotic Vera they knew at work.

"I sent Greg out to the pub for an hour or so. No, nothing's wrong," she said in response to Alice's raised eyebrows. "He fusses over me too much. Besides, I could do with some girl talk."

It was warm in the kitchen although the window was open and there was an appetising smell of cooking meat. "Not my doing," Vera said when Alice commented on it. "I'm useless with lumps of raw flesh. Salad's about my limit."

There was just room for a small formica table and two chairs in the kitchen. If Vera entertained she took two folding chairs from the hall cupboard and everyone had to squeeze in. From where they sat, below the level of the window, all that was visible through it was a pale sky. Traffic sounds were muted and Alice found it peaceful in an odd sort of way.

"Open this, will you?" Vera handed her a bottle of wine and a corkscrew. "I dare not risk it yet, especially if the cork's a tight fit."

Alice poured the wine. "You're different," she said as she handed Vera a glass. She tilted her head to one side and said with her impish grin, "I can't make out what it is, but something's changed."

"No war paint."

"No, it's more than that. It's you."

"All right, I give in. It's Greg." Vera paused and sipped her wine. "He wants us to live together. Actually, he wants us to get married, but after two goes at it I'm not sure I want to risk it again."

Alice watched with amazement as tears filled Vera's eyes. She had always believed her to be the least vulnerable person she had ever come across. "Whatever's the matter?"

"I'm scared, Alice. I'm terrified that if I agree, if we live together, it'll all start going wrong." She brushed the tears away impatiently, annoyed with herself. "Take no notice of me, it's my hormones playing up. Here, have another glass of wine."

"I don't know what to say. No, I don't mean about the wine," she added in response to Vera's raised eyebrows.

"I didn't think you'd refuse." Vera's tone was dry.

"You've got to do what's right for you, what feels right. It doesn't matter what anyone else says or thinks. I'm not really the one to give you advice, my love life hasn't been a resounding success lately."

"I know. We didn't say much, but we all knew how hard it must've been, finishing with Keith after all that time."

"Keith? I wasn't thinking of him."

"Oh? You'd better fill me in, young lady."

Pinkness rose over Alice's cheekbones. "I've been seeing James Winter for the past few weeks."

110

"You've what? My God, girl, how on earth did you manage to keep that to yourself?"

Alice shrugged. "Well, James didn't seem to have mentioned it to Jack, and, I, well, to be honest, I didn't think it would come to anything. After Keith I suppose I was being extra careful and I don't think I could've borne the teasing. Vera, you won't say anything, will you? I'd prefer it if people didn't know just yet."

"Of course I won't. But why do you say your love life isn't a success? I shouldn't think you could do much better than James Winter."

"I thought he just enjoyed my company, but that he didn't fancy me. He didn't touch me, you see, not at first."

"Not at all?" Vera was incredulous. In her experience keeping men's hands off her was the problem.

"No. But I see now that he was taking it slowly. He told me his last girlfriend ditched him, obviously he didn't want to risk it happening again. Anyway, he's kissed me now."

"And?"

"And what?" Alice laughed. It was typical of Vera to want to know all the details.

"Is he good? At kissing, I mean?"

"Good enough," Alice told her without expanding further.

"Ah, here's Greg. He wasn't long."

"It seems he can't keep away from you. Hi," she said when Greg came in. She had only previously seen him in a suit. He looked more boyish than ever in a checked shirt and black cords. The effect was heightened by the light brown hair which flopped over his forehead. Less boyish was the slight paunch which rested over his waistband.

111

"Hello, Alice. Has she told you?"

"I have," Vera answered defiantly.

"Good. Any chance of a glass of that wine?" It was Greg who tested the casserole and put it back in the oven. "The lady of the house sees to the vegetables," he said. "I've managed to teach her that much."

"You know I'm hopeless in the kitchen department." Vera never hesitated to defend herself and smiled at Greg in a way which suggested she had gone as far as she was prepared to with matters of a culinery nature.

"Keep me informed about James," Vera said when she showed her to the door. "And I promise I won't say a word to anyone, not even Greg."

It was, she realised, decision time. Alice was quite right, she must do whatever her head and heart dictated. Vera had no illusions where romance was concerned, it was a fleeting thing, the long term was more important. Watching Greg lay the table she suddenly arrived at a decision. "Greg?"

He looked up, frowing at the intensity of her expression. "What is it?"

"I've got something to tell you."

Myriad thoughts flashed through his mind. Had something gone wrong with the operation? A hysterectomy, she had finally admitted, but had she lied? At least he understood the implications, that Vera would never have children. But supposing it was something worse, something he did not want to think about? Maybe she had come to a decision and no longer wanted to see him, perhaps had already met another man, one who was more fun and who did not want to tie her down. Or was it simply that she felt she could not agree to marry him because she would be depriving him of the chance of more children?

If that was so he had to convince her he didn't care, that all he wanted was to be with her, on any terms.

Taking the chair opposite she said quietly, "I haven't been strictly honest with you." She took a deep breath. "I'm not thirty-nine. No. Wait." Greg had let out a bellow of laughter. "I'm older than you: I'm forty-three."

"I know," he said, still smiling.

"You know?" She pulled back her hair with both hands as if to see him more clearly. "But how can you?"

"Simple mathematics. You once let slip that you left school in 1968. Well assuming you were sixteen at the time, it makes you at least that."

"Why didn't you say something?"

"Because it doesn't really matter. I'm hardly a toy boy, Vera, you're only a year older. Watch up, the carrots are boiling over."

It doesn't matter, she thought as she got up to turn down the gas. It really doesn't matter to him what age I am. She knew then that soon she would tell him she would live with him. She would not give up the flat immediately if it was possible to keep it on, but it was a start. She would take it from there.

On Friday, James and Alice walked to a local pub and listened to some jazz. "I don't mind it," James said.

"What's you favourite sort of music?" Alice asked him, curiously.

He shrugged. "It's all the same to me, no favourites, just depends on the mood I'm in."

But Alice noticed he was tapping his foot and was pleased he wasn't bored. Liz hated jazz but Alice would sometimes go with her father if there was a band performing at his local.

113

"I can't see you tomorrow," James told her later, when he walked her home, "but I'll see you Sunday, as arranged. What kind of flowers does you mother like?"

"There's no need for that, she'll be just as pleased to see you empty-handed."

She did not mind having Saturday to herself: she needed to do some serious food shopping. Josie was going with her and they would also window shop, and have a coffee somewhere, and her library books needed returning if she wasn't to pay a fine.

It was raining on Sunday, heavy rain, which showed no sign of abating. The trees dripped and the daffodils and crocuses in Josie's window box were bent double and sodden. Alice was not sorry James had a car.

Liz must have been watching for them because the door was open as soon as they opened the gate of the tiny front garden.

"Pleased to meet you, Mrs Powell," James said.

"Liz, please," she replied. "And I've met you before, you know. Several times, when you were little."

"Ah, when my ears stuck out."

"Yes." She laughed in spite of all her reservations and accepted the flowers he had, after all, brought her, along with a bottle of wine.

Alice was amused at her father's *bonhomie*, his exaggerated efforts to make James feel at home. With a frown she went to the kitchen to help Liz. But what was James's home like? She had still not been to his flat, nor did she know where it was.

The food was delicious. Liz had excelled herself with a joint of pork, on which the crackling was perfect. The roast potatoes were crisp and the vegetables just cooked

114

enough to retain their full flavour. Derek had also bought wine. They drank that first, knowing James's would be superior, thereby saving the best until last.

"No more, thanks." James put a hand over his glass. "I've got the car."

Liz refilled the other glasses. His father, she recalled, had had no such qualms as a young man, but things were different in those days, and Jack had been a bit wild then. Ruth had changed him, for the better. She was the ideal wife for Jack and, despite everything, she knew he loved her.

"Market research? Quite big business these days," Derek said, pouring cream on his apple pie.

But James refused to be drawn out over his job. Instead he asked about Derek's work.

"Hardly exciting, but I enjoy the freedom. Our son, Mark's a bit the same, works for the electricity board but every day's different. Schools, private houses, hospitals, outside work. He's all over the place in his van. That's how Alice met Keith, he's—" he caught Liz's warning look but it was too late.

"James knows about Keith," Alice interrupted quickly, and smiled at both men.

They did not stay long. Alice knew her father wanted to watch the football on TV, and James did not like sport. It wasn't only that. The atmosphere had not been comfortable and it was not down to James or even her father's tactless comment. It had been Liz. She had seemed on edge, as if she did not really want them to be there.

"'Bye, Mum, it was as delicious, as always," she said.

James also thanked her. Alice couldn't fault him

on his manners and he had tried hard to draw Liz out.

"'She's a great cook," he said, as they drove back to her place.

"I know. Do you want to come in for coffee?"

"No thanks. I promised I'd help Dad saw up some logs for the fire." He shook his head. "I don't know why he doesn't get them delivered but he insists he prefers cutting them himself. Alice, I've got a lot of things to see to this week, you'll find out what they are at the weekend. I won't be able to see you until Friday. Is that all right?"

"That's fine," she replied lightly. Though a little disappointed, she would meanwhile, go somewhere with Josie, perhaps have an after work drink with Marg and try to find out what was bothering her mother.

Liz was also busy that week but they arranged that Alice would call in on Friday before she went out. Alice had three hours between leaving work and meeting James so there was plenty of time.

"Dad's out, I'm cooking for the freezer," Liz explained, when Alice arrived to find all the work surfaces covered with utensils and meat in various stages of preparation. "Thank goodness I only need to do this once a month."

"Shall I make you a coffee?" Alice asked.

"Love one." Her mother smiled, gratefully.

"Mum, you don't mind me seeing James, do you?" Alice ventured.

"Mind? Why on earth should I?" Liz hooked her hair back with her little fingers; her hands were bloody from the stewing steak she was dicing. She avoided Alice's eyes.

116

"No reason," Alice replied. "Can I do anything to help?"

"No, there's a method here believe it or not," Liz joked, relieved that Alice had changed the subject.

Alice placed a mug of black coffee beside her mother and poured milk into her own.

"Alice, those telephone calls, they've been bothering me. Dad and I are worried about you."

"No need. They've stopped. So have those to Vera and Marg." So that's what it was all about, Alice thought. Her mother was tense, presumably because of what she had said about the phone calls. Perhaps she ought not to have mentioned them. "I must go in a minute," she said, "I've got to wash and change yet."

"Do you want to borrow an umbrella?" Liz nodded towards the window through which they could see the sodden garden. But the heavy showers had turned into a fine drizzle.

"No thanks. I'm going to wash my hair anyway."

"Give us a ring over the weekend, or Monday if you're busy."

"I will," Alice promised.

But her mother did not seem her usual self, she thought, after she had kissed her goodbye and began making her way back to the flat.

Alice was only just ready in time and James was always punctual. She put on a raincoat over the tan pinafore and watched from the window for his car. Two girls from across the street, dressed up for an evening out, scurried into a waiting taxi. Other pedestrians were making for the newsagent's for their Friday night cans of beer or sweets or a video but the kebab house was empty. Their trade came later. "Am I allowed to know what the surprise is yet?" she asked James when he arrived.

"Absolutely not." And with a warning grin, he refused to discuss it further.

They went to an American-type restaurant which served cocktails as well as beer and where the burgers bore little resemblance to the ones purchased from fast food chains. They were thick and full of meat and tasted delicious. No matter how she phrased it, Alice could not persuade James to tell her anything more about the coming weekend.

"How's work been?" he asked, trying to keep her off the subject.

"Not bad this week, no catastrophes at any rate. Still, I'll be glad when Vera's back."

"I bet you will. Dad been tearing his hair out, has he? He used to terrify me when I was a kid. Not that there was anything to be scared of, once he'd shouted or said his piece, that was the end of it. He's not a man to bear grudges."

"I know." Alice was quiet, concentrating on the salad which came with the burger as she thought about Jack. Could it have been him? He had easy access to their telephone numbers and although he had not said anything, it was quite obvious he was under some sort of pressure at the moment. But it was not worth thinking about now, especially as the calls and letters appeared to have stopped.

"Sweet?" James was asking.

"I couldn't possibly." Alice had seen the large portions other diners were receiving.

"Ah, that's how you keep that beautiful figure."

Her eyes widened. It was the first direct compliment

James had given her, though it was only as he spoke that she realised it.

They sat talking over coffees and the remains of the wine then James said they ought to leave. There was only one other couple in the place and the staff were beginning to clear up.

He drove her home and saw her to her door. When he kissed her, Alice noticed he was less hesitant this second time and she was further encouraged into believing it was going to work out between them. "Until tomorrow then," he said, teasingly, and turned to leave.

"Wait! What shall I wear?"

James gripped his chin in an attitude of contemplation then smiled enigmatically. "Anything you like," he said and got into the car before without giving her a chance to ask anything else. Despite herself, Alice felt a thrill of excitement. She enjoyed surprises.

The pleasant stage between wakefulness and knowing sleep was imminent was shattered when Alice's telephone rang. "Yes?" she snapped shortly.

"Alice. Oh, Alice. What a bitch you are."

She froze. "Wait . . ." but the caller had hung up. Almost in tears of fear and frustration on top of tiredness, Alice sat down at the table and wrote a short list of everyone who had her new number; her parents, her brother, Jack Winter, Phyllis Greenslade – but Phyllis had left now. Though she could have made a note of their numbers and taken them with her. But surely that low voice did not belong to Phyllis?

Mr Green had not done at all well in the angling competition but he was not despondent. His nature was

119

such that he could sit happily on the bank of a river or stream under a dripping umbrella or a cloudless sky for hours on end, his mind devoid of thought as he enjoyed his surroundings and the peaceful solitide. He knew he was no intellectual, but he was a contented man, happy in his job and his lodgings and happier still when fishing. He found nothing more relaxing than being near water and the occasional plop as a fish rippled the surface, even if few of them ever ventured near his lines.

Eleven years ago, when he first moved in with her, Hilary Green had worried that Marg might expect a little more from him than the weekly rent but, wordlessly, she had managed to convey that their arrangement was on strict business terms. That was then. Their proximity had ensured that, given their proclivity to politeness and consideration, they had become friends. There were, however, times when they were both grateful to be alone.

Marg had been more worried about the disgusting letters she and her friends had been receiving that she had allowed him to believe but he hadn't made any fuss, realising she prefered not to talk about it with him. It was an embarrassing subject between two people of the opposite sex. Perhaps her age had something to do with it, he could remember his mother being short tempered when she was in her fifties.

The continuous fine drizzle did not deter him. Hilary Green, protected by waterproofs and thigh-length boots, continued to fish long after the other competitors had gone home. It had crossed his mind that he was a little in love with Marjorie Finch, not that he would ever do anything about it, and that he was genuinely concerned for her welfare. It was an intriguing idea to a man who had shown little interest in women over the years but Marg, he was sure, would laugh outright at the suggestion if he told her.

I can dream, he told himself, knowing that his happiness lay that way, that the reality would be a lot different. To his amazement his line gave a small jerk. Surprised and inordinately gratified, he forgot all about Marg as he reeled in his catch.

James lay on his bed and waited for morning, so excited he knew he would not be able to sleep without his pills. Impossible to believe Larry had come up with the idea and had been responsible for organising it although it had not been as simple as it had first appeared. But Alice would be so happy.

Though Larry had set it all up, he had never been there. This was important: they had to be safe from Larry at least until Alice had agreed to marry James. And she would; James knew that now. He had sensed how much closer they were becoming and was pleased he had not rushed things.

"Alice." He spoke her name aloud. "Alice Winter. Pretty, little Alice." He had money. He would dress her, cosset her and make her life easy. It was obvious she would be a devoted wife. No children, though, he thought, unsure of his reasons.

The small alarm clock beside the bed ticked away the minutes. He must sleep; he had a fairly long drive tomorrow. At one-fifteen he went to the bathroom and took one of the sleeping tablets he had been prescribed for his frequent bouts of insomnia . . .

The light filtering through the loose-weave curtains Liz had made, added to Alice's anticipation. A thin, yellow rectangle of sunshine fell across the carpet where she had not drawn them properly together. In the kitchen she made instant coffee and drank it while she ran a bath. Half an hour later most of her clothes were scattered over the bed as she tried to decide on an appropriate outfit for her mystery day out with James. Appropriate for what though? Letting her hair dry naturally, she fluffed it up with her fingers every so often until it formed little peaks around her face. Make-up, she decided, still in her dressing gown, then inspiration'll come to me.

Jeans were out because they might be going somewhere smart. But then James would have warned her. She recalled his words: Anything you like, it won't matter. An unsolvable mystery, but there was only an hour to wait until he was due to arrive.

Finally, but still unsure, she chose a black skirt which fitted snugly to just above the knees then gradually swirled out. Tucked into this was a black, square-necked cotton top and over this she wore a grey silky shirt as a jacket. The shirt had been Liz's, as were several items of her clothing. If the venue for this mystery outing was informal, the shirt could be taken off; if not, it was smart enough to pass almost anywhere. It was the best she could do.

Alice had just hung up the discarded clothes when James arrived.

"What is it, Jack?"

He turned around and saw that Ruth was studying him thoughtfully. "Nothing," he replied.

"And it's nothing that's been keeping you awake at night? It's more than the threat of competition from Cousins, isn't it?"

122

"I'm sorry, have I been disturbing you?"

"Jack, tell me, please." She crossed the room and stood by his side at the open French windows which looked out over the slope of the garden. The heads of the daffodils around the bases of trees planted in the lawn were brown and shrivelled; the gardener would remove them in a day or so, but patches of tulips lent bright colour.

All this, he thought, a lovely home, healthy kids, a beautiful wife, it's all mine. But maybe it was too much; maybe this dreadful turn of events had happened to redress the balance because no one should have too much . . . "I can't tell you, Ruthie," he said at last. "This is something I have to deal with myself."

Jack had no idea of the extent of his wife's knowledge.

He was due to play golf at ten-thirty and was dressed appropriately, the slacks, rather than the jacket, checked, a gold-coloured polo shirt and soft, brown leather shoes. Ruth was to join him at lunchtime. He did not want to go but knew that staying at home worrying would not change anything. There was an alternative to waiting for Alice to tire of James but the risks involved were excessive. "It'll be all right," he said reassuringly before kissing Ruth on the cheek and picking up his car keys. "I'll see you about one."

Ruth remained staring out at the garden, preoccupied, not seeing the birds busy with their nests. She had little to do that day, other than to change into a linen dress ready for lunch. Her auburn hair was held back in a wooden clasp but it was tugging at her head. She removed it but the dull ache remained, caused, she knew, by something else.

James was a worry, but one she could cope with. It was this other thing which concerned her more, what it would do to Jack, to them all as a family if it

123

was openly admitted. She had known, of course, and had even understood but the repercussions now could be disastrous.

"Liz?"

"Sorry, I was miles away."

"Come here." Derek took Liz's hand and pulled her closer. "Why don't we have a night out, just the two of us? We don't seem to have had a free Saturday for ages."

"Yes, OK," she replied, slowly.

"That doesn't sound very enthusiastic. Loosing interest in your old man?" Derek teased.

"Of course not." Liz managed a smile.

"You're not still worried about Alice, are you? She told us all that nonsense has stopped."

"I can't help worrying. I am her mother."

Derek was satisfied that this was the cause of his wife's subdued mood and left it at that. They made the most of the sunshine and sat reading in the sheltered back garden until Liz went in to have a bath and get ready for their evening out. She was determined to be cheerful even though her anxiety was increasing and she felt a debilitating sense of foreboding.

James opened the sunroof before he started the engine. The breeze was pleasant as he and Alice drove along.

"Am I allowed to know now?" she quizzed.

"No. Not until we get there."

They continued in silence as James manoeuvred through the traffic. She realised he was a man who did not like to talk when he was driving, and it suited her. As they passed by, she felt no envy of the shoppers with their bulging supermarket carriers or the mothers with

124

prams and pre-school children who struggled through the busy town centre.

James could hardly control his own excitement and his anticipation was infectious. "It wasn't easy to set this up so quickly," he told her. "But you're really going to enjoy it."

"Oh, James, don't tease."

He laughed. Alice realised it was not a sound she had heard before. It was a strange, deep-throated laugh.

By eleven they had cleared the outskirts of the town and James took the coast road for several miles before turning left, confident of the direction.

The sun, through the glass of the side-window, was warm. Alice removed her grey overshirt and put it on the back seat along with James's jacket. Perhaps a black top and skirt were too wintery for the weather. However, it was too late now, and James had not said she was unsuitably dressed. He was in chinos and an open-necked shirt.

Her mind went back to the latest anonymous telephone call, but she was not going to mention it; nothing must spoil the day. Besides, how could she say to James that she suspected there was a possibility his father might be behind it all? Her thoughts drifted; tomorrow she must go to the launderette, and, she must make her final decision on which course she was going to take. She had pared it down to business management or full-time training as a beautician. Already she was more or less certain it would be the latter as long as she could get finance arranged. Josie had pointed out that she could set up on her own if she didn't want to work for anyone or take a job in a hotel or on a cruise liner. Alice was so wrapped up in the possibilities of what her future held that she took little notice of where they were going. James stuck to B roads where the hedges were beginning to thicken and the buds of the overhanging trees were pale green fronds. Crops were higher in the fields and the countryside looked fresh and clean after the dreary months of winter.

"Lunch," James said, as he pulled in beside a pub. It was a large, rambling building, set back from the road, and presumably got its trade from passing motorists as there were no houses within view. The parking area at the side was three-quarters full, the weather having brought people out.

Alice was now seeing another side of James. Now that things had become a little more physical, he seemed more confident. His manner was positive; he was in control, all signs of insecurity had vanished. And he was more ready to smile. It suited him, she thought, watching his strong hands as he paid for their drinks.

"There's plenty of room outside," the landlord told them.

"We're fine here, thanks." James answered for both of them although Alice would have prefered to sit in the sun. He carried their drinks to a dim corner and handed Alice a menu. "Just a bar snack. We'll be eating properly later."

She shook her head and sighed. Still he wasn't going to tell her their destination. An egg salad was Alice's choice. James ordered a Stilton ploughman's but when it arrived he merely picked at it.

"Would you like another drink?" Alice asked him when they had finished eating.

"No." James's terse reply startled her. He had only had a half-pint of bitter. "No," he said again, more gently. "We have to make a move now."

She did not expect much conversation once they were back in the car but was puzzled because it was already afternoon and they were still travelling. It was going to be a long day. Now and then she turned to watch his profile and noticed the perspiration on his brow. She hoped he was not going to be ill again. Alice bit her lip; it was a completely selfish thought, she chided herself.

High hedges soon surrounded them again and Alice had a sense of *déjà vu*; the terrain seemed familiar.

"James!" She jerked forward, and the seat belt tightened and threw her back into her seat. James had taken a bend too fast and had to brake suddenly to avoid an oncoming car. It was unlike him, he was a careful driver. He muttered something which she did not hear and she thought it best not to disturb his concentration further by saying anything herself.

Altogether they had been driving for a little over two hours. Once he seemed calmer Alice asked if he could now tell her where they were heading.

"You'll see. We're almost there," he replied. "You'll see it all soon."

Shortly afterwards he made a left turning. The road narrowed, twigs scratched the bodywork of the car then the lane became no more than a rutted track. James pulled off the road between some trees. "We're here," he said with satisfaction.

Alice got out of the car, pleased to be able to stretch her legs. There was a peaceful stillness around them — not even birdsong disturbed the silence. Opposite was a five-barred gate but from where she stood Alice could not see where it led as the ground sloped away behind the hedge.

James opened the gate and beckoned her through

it with a nod of his head. About eighty yards away stood a stone cottage enclosed on its other three sides by drystone walling. The garden was an overgrown wilderness: brambles and thistles had taken over from roses and delphiniums. It would have been idyllic with a bit of work.

Alice was not sure what she was supposed to say. Although she had had no idea what the surprise was going to be, it certainly was not this.

"The garden's a mess, but the inside's terrific. Come on," James encouraged.

She thought she understood. James had not taken her to his flat but he was making up for it now. He had bought this place and wanted to show it to her before he moved in. It was very flattering. They made their way, single file, down the path which was weed-free, and he unlocked the door with a large, old-fashioned key he took from the jacket over his arm.

The coolness inside was a welcome relief after the stickiness of the car. The door opened straight into the living room which had a flagstone floor covered with a couple of mats. The sofa and one armchair were appropriately covered in the same chintz as the curtains and the few other items of furniture were of solid wood and although they were old, were not antiques. Another door led to the kitchen, James told her.

"Come and see upstairs, first," he said, leading the way up a twisted, wooden staircase leading from the living room. There were two bedrooms, both furnished in a floral fabric which Alice found a bit twee but was too polite to say so. The views were lovely: nothing but fields and trees and grazing cattle in the distance and the steeple of a church which must belong to the nearest village.

"It's really nice, James," Alice said, seeing his expectant expression.

"The bathroom's downstairs," James continued. "Obviously a more recent extension. Kitchen next."

No alterations had been made to the kitchen's original design. It was square, and also flagstoned, but the sink unit was new and there were all the usual appliances. It suddenly occurred to Alice that the place was fully furnished. Had James chosen everything or had he brought someone else in to do it?

"Look." He opened cupboards which were stocked with dry goods and the fridge which was full. From it he took a bottle of champagne then two glasses from a cupboard. "The freezer's in here." It just fitted into the good-sized cupboard and was also fully stocked. "And that door leads to the bathroom, which I'll show you later. But first . . ." He expertly uncorked the champagne and poured it.

"How long have you had this little secret?" Alice questioned.

"Not long. Here." Alice took the glass. "Here's to our future," he said.

"Ours?" Alice repeated, overwhelmed.

"Oh, yes, Alice. Ours."

Her hand trembled slightly as she sipped the drink. It was ice-cold, not at all sweet, and she guessed it was expensive. "Cheers," she said, wondering why she found his manner suddenly somehow threatening.

"There's no garden furniture so we can't sit outside," James explained. "The back's in a better state than the front, though."

They took their drinks and the bottle through to the living room. The sun was already lowering in the sky. Orange rays fanned out and were reflected in the mullioned windows, one of which James had opened.

Sitting at the polished oak table in the window, Alice saw how blissful it would be to live somewhere like this, except that its remote location made it impractical for work. Presumably James had bought it as a weekend retreat. And yet, peaceful as it should have been, there was something not quite right. Like her mother, Alice had a sixth sense when it came to buildings: some she could walk into and not wish to remain; others seemed to have an atmosphere of security which enveloped her. Here, there was no aura of tragedy, it was not the cottage itself which was making her uneasy. In which case, she reasoned, it had to be James. He was gazing out of the window and she wondered if he was picturing the garden as it could be in the future. Feeling her eyes on him he turned and smiled.

Alice suddenly had a flash of insight, which didn't make her any more comfortable. So that was it, the big seduction scene: a country cottage, plenty of food, and champagne . . . Did James need all these accompaniments? Or did he think she did? And why did it all seem so wrong? For the moment however, there was little she could do about it. In her excitement she had been unusually stupid, she had not taken note of the direction in which they had come and now had no idea where she was if she needed to get public transport home. She bit her lip as she realised it was a peculiar thing to be thinking. Surely she trusted James not to force her to do anything she wasn't ready for?

James had topped up her glass and refilled his own which he had again emptied, Alice noticed. On previous occasions he had had only one or two drinks when

130

he was driving. At this rate he would be incapable of getting them home this evening. She could drive herself, of course. She had taken, and passed her test at the first opportunity. However, she was only used to driving her mother's runaround, which she borrowed in emergencies – a small Fiesta, so she did not relish the thought of handling James's large, executive model, especially if it was dark and she was unfamiliar with the road. But if she was right, and this was a seduction scene, James had probably planned for them to stay the night. Though why had he not said they would be away overnight so she could bring some toiletries and a change of clothes? There was no choice but to sit back, relax and try to enjoy herself, Alice concluded. She wondered if her nervousness stemmed from the unconnected strange events which had been taking place recently.

When James tried to pour her more champagne she put her hand over her glass. "No," she said, "I've had enough." He shrugged and carried on drinking.

"Do you really like the place, Alice?"

She nodded. "I do. It's lovely. You can get away from it all here, it's so quiet."

"That's what Larry thought."

"Larry? Oh, your friend. How is he now? You said he was worrying you."

James smiled. "He's fine. There won't be any more problems as far as Larry is concerned."

"When am I going to meet him?" Alice asked.

James, on his way to the kitchen, spun around. "Never. Don't even ask," he snapped.

Shocked, Alice remained seated at the table. She finally allowed herself to admit that she was becoming frightened; that now she thought about it, she hardly knew James. He had not let her get to know him. His job, for example: he had told her parents he was in market research. He had made light of it, offering no explanation as to exactly what it was he did and Jack had never discussed his work in the way he did his other children's occupations. Maybe she should telephone someone just to be on the safe side. Unless James had told anyone of his plans, no one at all knew where she was. But looking around she saw there was no telephone. Perhaps there was one in the kitchen, or even one of the bedrooms.

"James?' she called anxiously.

"You sit there and relax," he called back. "I'm cooking us a meal. I'm really going to spoil you."

Such ordinary words, depicting an ordinary activity made Alice think she had been worrying unnecessarily. The sun had dropped lower and a cool breeze stirred the weeds which she could smell through the open window. She told herself again her unease was ridiculous as she concentrated on her surroundings. It was a way of preventing stirrings of panic, originating somewhere in her stomach, from rising.

It's a comfortable room, she decided, noticing the discreet radiators against the walls. There was also an open fireplace which looked as if it had recently been used and the stone walls were uneven which added to the quaintness.

James came in carrying cutlery and condiments. "Can I help you?" she asked.

"Oh, no, little Alice. You are my guest." More harmless, pleasant words, but this time they seemed menacing.

James seemed to have an endless supply of wine. He produced a very dry white to go with the first course.

"Go on," he insisted when Alice said she didn't want any. "We're doing things in style tonight."

He poured some anyway and Alice took a small sip and stared at the glistening black caviar on her plate.

"Is something wrong?" James enquired.

"No, nothing. It's just that I've never had caviar before." She smiled tentatively and tasted it. As she had told him during another conversation, there was nothing she would not eat and she had always wanted to try the exclusive sturgeon roe. But the conditions weren't right. Not here somehow; not with James. The fishy taste was strong and the texture glutinous, yet Alice knew if she were elsewhere, with someone else, she would have enjoyed it.

James had already finished the rest of the bottle of wine and stood up to clear the plates. So far the alcohol did not seem to be affecting him, except that his smile was more fixed, more of a leer, and his eyes were a little glassy.

Red wine accompanied the venison. Alice had to admit he was a good cook, but she was feeling light-headed after the glass of red wine James insisted she drink.

"There's no dessert," he said apologetically, slurring his words fractionally. "I know you don't usually want one. There's cheese, though."

"No thanks. I'm fine." Alice smiled. "It was delicious. Thank you. Now I'll wash up." She made a move to leave the table.

"No." James clamped his hand firmly on her arm. "Leave it."

A shiver ran through her at his touch. She wanted to pull away, to get out of there and go home to her flat, even, she thought, feeling like a small child, to her parents'. One thing was certain, however the evening turned out, she would not be sharing a bed with James. "All right," she said, going along with his mood. "We can always do them later."

She received no acknowledgement of her remark because James had picked up the wine bottle and slopped the remaining contents into his glass, spilling some on the table where the ruby liquid separated into globules on the polished wood.

Conversation had run out and Alice tried hard to think of a subject to get him talking; to sober him up a little. Watching him, she realised he seemed to have forgotten her presence, had, perhaps, had so much to drink he no longer knew what he was doing. The dishes remained on the table but she was too scared to do anything about it.

Time had become meaningless. How long was it since James had picked her up? Alice's hands lay in her lap. She pushed back her cuff without drawing attention to the movement and glanced at her watch. Nine-fifteen. At least, that's what she thought it said. The room had darkened rapidly. Were they, she wondered, to sit here in silence in the dark? "James? Could we have a light on, please?" Alice knew there could be no attempt to leave that night.

James, opposite her at the table, got to his feet and fumbled with the switch of a table lamp then staggered out in the direction of the kitchen. Alice sighed inwardly when he returned with another bottle of wine but the only consolation was that if he drank it, he would surely pass out. This time she was not offered a glass and she was pleased. There were two bedrooms, she would sleep in whichever he did not occupy, if he made it upstairs at all, and she would

134

remain fully-clothed, ready to leave as soon as it was daylight.

Once or twice sounds escaped from James's lips but Alice was unsure whether they were spoken thoughts or words directed at her. Either way, he did not seem to require an answer. Half-way through the red wine James's head dropped onto his chest. Minutes later he placed his arms on the table, overturning the pepper-mill as he did so. He rested his head on his arms and slept.

Very quietly Alice went upstairs, wincing as the boards creaked beneath her feet. In the smallest bedroom she wedged the back of a chair she found in the corner under the handle of the door before laying, shivering, under the duvet.

She slept fitfully for a few hours, waking at intervals, afraid James might come bursting in. The chair was light, with a woven cane seat and a curved back but at least it would make a noise as it broke if James exerted pressure on the door.

A grey dawn light filtered into the room. Alice opened her eyes. Downstairs there were noises. The chair was still wedged under the door-handle and, with the daylight, she felt vaguely foolish. James had let his hair down, drunk too much, nothing more than that had happened. She tidied her hair with her hands in front of the dressing-table mirror and let herself out, carefully replacing the chair where she had found it.

"Good morning," James said formally when she appeared in the kitchen doorway. "Coffee?"

"Yes, please." Alice watched him fill the container of the coffee machine with shaking hands. Other than that there were no signs of a hangover. Nor was there any explanation or apology.

"Something to eat?"

"No. I'm still full from last night." This remark did not invoke a response either. She sat silently watching the sky lighten and listening to the gurgling sounds as the water ran through the filter. Her mouth watered as the rich aroma of coffee filled the kitchen.

James placed a mug in front of her. Alice thanked him and took a welcome sip. "What time are we leaving?" she asked.

"Leaving? Who said anything about leaving?"

"But, James . . ."

"There are no buts now, Alice, only our future." His brown eyes appeared black in the intensity of his gaze. He stood, towering over Alice, a figure to be feared. How had she ever imagined she might be falling in love with him?

"I have things to do," she said quietly, "and there's work tomorrow."

"Work." His tone was scornful. "You can forget work. My father is your boss and I've squared it with him. He's not expecting you in."

Alice was furious. How dare anyone try to run her life for her. And as for Jack, she could not believe he would go along with such a thing without at least mentioning it to her. So he had known all along. "Your reasons may be well intentioned, but I do not allow people to tell me what I will or won't do. No one makes arrangements like this without consulting me first." Her icy voice was ineffectual, James merely bared his teeth in what she took to be a smile. It made her feel physically sick.

Alice tried to recall what had happened on Friday

evening. Jack had patted her on the shoulder and made some comment about having a good weekend, but he said that to everyone, every Friday. Something told her that James was lying, that Jack had no idea where she was.

She stood up, leaving her coffee, and went into the sitting-room where she took her jacket from where she had left it on the back of the settee and picked up her handbag. Back in the kitchen she faced James and said, "You can stay if you wish, but I'm leaving."

A sound escaped him, almost a giggle. Alice walked to the back door. It was locked and there was no key. Wondering if she was being melodramatic, she turned and stalked into the living-room and lifted the latch of the front door. That, too, was locked.

"James, this is ridiculous. Please unlock the door."

"No, Alice. You're mine. I want you here with me."

Terror rendered her incapable of movement. There was a finality in his words, enough to frighten anybody. But her stomach muscles contracted and he knees went weak because she had heard those same words before, spoken with the same voice.

She needed to think, to stop the panic which was rising. Was it possible to climb out of the window and run as fast as she could to the main road. No, he was so much taller than herself, he would catch her in seconds. Besides, she realised with a jolt, the windows were all now closed and there were security locks on them, the type that required a key to open them. Naturally, the property being so isolated, the previous owners would have had them fitted, especially if they only used it occasionally. There was, she thought defeatedly, no point in trying other rooms, James would have left nothing to chance. And the windows themselves, with their leaded diamonds of glass, would be impossible to smash. Drawing upon courage she did not know she possessed, she decided she would simply wait. There had to be a time when she was alone or, if he repeated last night's performance, James fell asleep.

"Want some, little Alice?" James was holding a bottle towards her invitingly.

She shook her head. Fine, let him drink himself into another stupor, she would find a key, perhaps the car keys too, and get away. It was, she saw, to be a waiting game, and her stubbornness and patience would stand her in good stead.

"I haven't told you about Larry, have I?"

"No." Good, let him talk. As long as he didn't touch her.

"We've been like that for years." James crossed two fingers to demonstrate their closeness. "Since I first went to boarding school, in fact."

"What was it like, being away at school?" The game had begun.

"OK." But he looked away, shutting himself off from her. "All this, it was Larry's idea," he eventually said.

"What was?"

"This." He waved a hand to encompass the whole cottage. Alice waited. "You see, I didn't know how to go about it, how to convince you that you belonged to me. I know you think so too, but you won't admit it. Even after what you did, what Larry saw you do, you can't deny you're meant to be with me. You're not like the others, I know that, Alice. I know you'll do the things I want."

"What things?" Her throat was tight. The alcohol was making him this way, that had to be the explanation. His face had altered, he was no longer handsome. The phone

138

calls and the letters, it was James, not his father, who was responsible. She knew that now. Why had it not occurred to her before? And what if he intended carrying out those threats?

James downed the wine and came over to her. He placed a hand either side of her head and when his slack mouth made contact with hers she gagged and pulled away. "No. James, I want to know, what things?"

"You bitch." Alice flinched but he did not hit her. Spittle clung to the corner of his mouth and, close up, she saw his eyes were bloodshot. "Larry was wrong. Larry said to take you somewhere where we could be alone and everything would work out. He knows about these things, he never has any trouble." He leant forward, his face inches from her own and she could smell his rancid breath. "Larry just takes what he wants. He raped someone once." James stopped. He was shaking. He backed away with an expression of horror on his face and reached for the bottle and poured another drink. When he turned back he was smiling.

The weather had brightened up again. Liz Powell decided she had done her share of cooking over the past couple of weeks. This Sunday a salad would suffice, especially as they had planned to use the day catching up on all those jobs which had been neglected for far too long. Derek was out in the small back garden. She watched him through the window, back bent, sweating, as he dug and cleared the ground. He had no real interest in flowers or vegetables, Liz saw to all that, but he liked digging, he claimed it was satisfying to see a clean piece of earth and it helped to stretch his muscles after all the miles he did in the car each week.

She knew every inch of his body, every line of his face and, she suspected, most of the thoughts which passed through his mind. They were a couple, they suited each other and were happier than most. All that marred things was the secret, the one stupid lapse and it worried her because she could not bear to see Derek hurt. He must have felt her gaze on him because he looked up and waved and made drinking motions with his hand.

Liz nodded and filled the kettle. He was a thoughtful man, he would drink his tea outside so as not to bring mud into the kitchen, and he would remove his boots when he finally did come in.

There had been no answer from Alice's phone. Perhaps she was out with James again, or, hopefully, one of her friends. She would not be in bed still, Alice had always been an early riser. Mark was a different matter, moaning and groaning as a child when she had to get him up for school, lying in bed until eleven or twelve when he was a teenager. Now he seemed to find no trouble in getting up for work but perhaps little Damien was responsible for that. Thank God, she thought, neither of mine were hyperactive.

"Thanks, love." Derek took his tea, strong with two sugars and sipped it. "The ground's just perfect." At his feet lay a pile of weeds; dandelions and thistles which always surived no matter what he did. At least he had got rid of the couch grass. "Did you get through?"

"No, she's out. I'll try again later."

"You've got to stop worrying, Liz. She told you the phone calls had stopped."

"I know. Are you sure you're happy with salad? You'll be hungry when you've finished."

140

"That'll be fine. Go and put your feet up, have a read or something."

"I just want to do the airing cupboard, then I will." She hesitated. "Derek?"

He studied her attractive face. Her dark hair needed washing, it was a little lank, but Liz would do it later, when she had done her tidying. She wasn't quite herself lately. She was listless and edgy but she had assured him nothing was wrong. "Derek, what?"

"Nothing."

"Chuck us out a couple of bin liners, would you?"

Liz went back to the kitchen. What she was doing was selfish, she was putting her own security ahead of everything else. Her priorities, she knew, were wrong, the other matter was of far more serious consequence. If only she could have a few hours alone, to think things through. There had to be a solution. But would she find one where nobody got hurt?

Stella Roberts stood in the doorway of the cramped room she insisted upon calling the lounge. Rebecca was lolling on the sofa, feet on the arm, watching an American cartoon on the television. Stella went firmly over to the set and switched it off.

"I was watching that." Rebecca chewed the ends of her hair.

"Not until you've made your bed and tidied your room."

"I don't feel like it."

Stella felt the warmth in her neck. If only Colin were here, Rebecca wouldn't dare speak to her like that. The irony was, if Colin still around, none of them would be in the poky flat. His absence had made her inadequacies clear. Although she had not known about the other side of him, things always ran smoothly when he was around. The house was never untidy and Martin and Rebecca behaved themselves. Did they blame her for his leaving? Did they miss him? They had not said so and she, in her own misery, had not thought to ask.

Rebecca strolled over and turned on the television. It was the final straw. Stella ripped the plug out of the wall and stood, blocking the screen. "It's time we had a talk. Where's Martin?"

"Out."

Yes, out with the layabouts he'd picked up with. Well, she'd start here and now. One at a time.

Rebecca Roberts, at fifteen, listened to her mother in astonishment. She didn't know she had it in her. Since Dad had gone her mother had been a push-over. She and Martin had more or less pleased themselves what they did.

"I'm trying to be both parents at once. Hasn't it occurred to you how hard it is for me? Instead of helping, you do less, both of you. Do you think I enjoy working in that place?" Stella sat down. The stream of words had exhausted her strength. "Do you miss your dad? she asked quietly.

"Sometimes. Do you?"

Stella's eyes narrowed. "Not really," she said, sounding surprised. "I did at first." She knew then that what she missed was his presence rather than the man himself, and the material things he had been able to provide. It was a chastening thought.

Rebbecca reluctantly went to change her sheets which now had to be taken to a launderette because there was

142

no washing machine and nowhere to put one if they could afford it. While she was in her bedroom, Stella, with grim satisfaction, removed the plug of the television from its wire. When the time came she would be able to replace it. She had learned a lot over the past months but what she had learned that morning was that not only were things different, but that they would never revert to what they had been. They might be different, she thought, but I can make them better.

She made a cup of tea and waited for Martin to come home.

Jack was glad that James was away for the weekend. If he was with friends in Wiltshire, it meant he wasn't with Alice. And that was good news. If a relationship was serious, you wanted to spend every bit of free time together and if James was to be away for both nights it looked as if it had started to go wrong.

"He's taken his own car, I hope. When's he due back?"

"He didn't say. You know what he's like, we only get the bare facts. Apparently someone he was at school with rang and asked him down. Some sort of weekend party. I didn't think such things still existed," Ruth said with a smile.

"Not my idea of fun. No chance to relax. Some of those kids he was at school with had parents who'd make us seem like the poor relations."

"I'm going into town," Ruth said. "Anything you want?"

"You could get me a box of my cigars, I'm nearly out. Tell old Price to put them on the monthly account."

Jack had not realised he was tense, but with the news

Ruth had imparted his stomach muscles unclenched. It was going to be all right.

Joan Wenton surprised Keith by being oversolicitous and making feeble attempts at jokes during the weekend. He was not sure if he disliked this more, or less than when she was complaining. Whatever had caused her change of mood she kept to herself.

Having alerted Jack Winter to the fact that James was seeing Alice, she knew there was nothing more to fear. Jack would put an end to it and Alice would come running back to Keith. That Jackie Pearce won't stand a chance, she thought, as bustled around preparing lunch and listened to a music station on the radio.

Even if she was mistaken in what she thought Liz Powell had almost confided all those years ago, Jack would not want his son to go about with a girl who worked on the shop floor.

Chapter Seven

Vera sat at her dressing-table applying her make-up. Greg's figure was reflected beside her as he watched with a frown. "Are you sure you're up to it? You know what the doctor said."

"Bugger the doctor. I can't stand another whole day of my own company. Besides, Jack's fixed it for me. And before you say another word, yes, I will take it easy and no, I won't go lifting anything. Now leave me in peace for five minutes."

Greg did as he was asked. Vera examined herself in the mirror, satisfied with what she saw, but the lines of fatigue would be back before the end of the day. She was not a hundred per cent fit yet and she knew she was not being sensible. However, she meant what she had said, she intended taking things very slowly. She shook her head to see the full effect of her newly tinted and permed spirals of hair. It had badly needed doing. "It takes some getting used to," she muttered, "having someone who really cares."

She had missed the company of Marg and Alice, and, now she thought about it, even Stella. It would be good to be back, to be a part of things again. "That's it. I'm ready. Let's go."

Greg dropped her at the bus-stop although he did not

have to be at work for another hour. Like a good omen, the sun continued to shine and glinted off the metal of cars and turned the pale buds of trees paler still.

"My God, there's Vera," Marg said to no one in particular.

Stella, in the seat in front, turned to look. "She shouldn't be back at work yet."

"No, but you know Vera; she won't be told." Marg saw Greg kiss her then say something. By the way Vera's curls were bobbing she was obviously reassuring him of something.

"Hello, love, nice to see you back. Feeling OK?" The driver leered appreciatively at her.

"Yeah. I feel like a new woman."

"So do I, but the wife won't let me."

"You don't look old enough to be married," Vera retorted, putting him in his place.

"You're a fool, Vera Langton, you know that, don't you?" Marg tutted.

"Don't you start, Marg, I've had all that from Greg already. Besides, I've spoken to Jack and he's put me on labels for a month so I'll be sitting down all day."

"Boring, but I suppose you'd be doing more at home."

"Anything exciting happened?"

Marg snorted. "Not unless you call a new line exciting. Fondant centres, nothing more revolting if you ask me. But Stella seems to like them."

Vera raised her eyebrows. Things had progressed if Stella was now part of the group. The woman herself twisted around and said she was pleased to see Vera back and hoped she was well. "If it was me, I'd have stayed at home and made the most of the weather."

"No garden," Vera replied.

146

"Nor have I, any more," Stella admitted. "But there's always the park."

"If you don't mind the dogs' mess." Marg pushed the curls back.

Vera felt a surge of energy. Good old Marg. And it was great to be back in the land of the living.

"They say we're in for a hot summer," Stella commented, still desperately trying to be liked. "But I usually take each day as it comes." She pursed her lips. That was her attitude to everything since her husband had left.

The bus pulled in through the factory gates above which was the large sign reminding them that this was Winter's Confectionery Company. Marg stood up and tucked the escaping corner of an emerald blouse into her trousers. Not until there was a heatwave would she relinquish trousers. Around her shoulders was a cable knit white cardigan.

"No Alice?" Vera suddenly noticed her absence. The others had been so surprised to see Vera at the stop they had not noticed.

"Perhaps she's decided to walk, now the weather's decent."

But she had not turned up by their tea break. Jack joined them in the canteen and reiterated his instructions to Vera. "If I catch you at anything you shouldn't be doing, I'll send you home. I mean it, Vera." Now warmer weather had arrived Jack's checked jackets had been cleaned and were hanging in polythene bags. They were replaced by a series of pale, striped ones, which, with his dark colouring, made the women comment that he looked like an Italian ice-cream seller. "Any of you know what's up with young Alice?" His tone was casual but he was more worried than they knew. "It's not like her to be

147

late." And he could not recall her having taken a day off before either.

"Perhaps she's rung the office and they've forgotten to tell you," Marg suggested. "She wouldn't just not turn up."

Jack left them to find out. The smile was no longer on his lips which were now pressed tightly together. The new girl in the office assured him there had been no message and was affronted he thought she had not be doing her job properly.

"She must be ill," Marg said to Vera when they broke for dinner. There was no opportunity to chat during the day because the labelling section was some distance away. "There's an awful lot of 'flu going about, perhaps she can't get to the phone. You know what it's like when it hits you hard, you're too weak to stand. Mr Green had a touch the other week but it didn't develop into anything."

"She seemed fine on Friday," Stella said.

"True, but things like that usually come on suddenly. If she's not in tomorrow, I'll call round and see her."

Vera struggled through the day but would not give in and admit she found it a bit much. The work itself was not in the least strenuous but just coping with a normal day had taken it out of her. No one was more relieved to get on the bus that evening.

Jack Winter watched from the window of his office which overlooked the entrance and saw his staff getting onto the coach. Three times he had tried Alice's home number but there was no reply. More than likely Marg was right: she was ill and had gone to her mother's to be looked after. He was fooling himself. Liz Powell would have rung to

148

let him know if Alice wasn't able to come in. He turned around and tapped out the digits which he now knew off by heart. Gnawing anxiety caused him to let it ring twenty odd times before he hung up. But James is with friends in Wiltshire, he thought, I'm over-reacting. And the lack of sleep did not help.

He got into his car and drove home. Monday nights were the best of the week. He and Ruth had a quiet drink then ate their meal. It was the one evening they made a point of neither entertaining nor going out, it was kept strictly for themselves and Ruth always cooked something special. They rarely watched television, preferring the radio or listening to music and Ruth was always content to read. Soon they would be able to sit outside in the evenings. He would have to get the barbecue out of the garage and clean it up a bit.

Ruth was in the kitchen stirring something on the cooker. Jack kissed the back of her neck and felt her soft hair tickle his face. "Is James back?"

"Not yet. He said he didn't know how long he was going for."

"Who are these friends?"

"Someone from school, apparently. I'm glad he's making an effort to socialise."

"Um. Are you ready for a drink yet?"

"Give me ten minutes then I can leave this to simmer."

Jack picked up the evening paper from where Ruth always left it, neatly folded on the hall table. His concentration was not good as he tried to remember the names of James's school friends. Damn it, he said to himself, I should've paid more attention. But he did not want to worry Ruth. Monday nights were sacrosanct. He was cursing himself for not having rung Liz Powell

149

before he left work, Ruth would wonder what the fuss was about if he did it from home. Tomorrow morning it was the first thing he would do.

The fates were against him. Jack could not recall the last time Ruth had been ill. She woke hot and flushed, with a thumping head and when she tried to stand, her legs buckled. "It's 'flu," she said weakly. "I'll be fine, Jack, you go to work." But he could not leave her as she was. Ruth was more important to him than anything, and she looked dreadful. He said he would sit with her until the doctor arrived.

"He won't do anything, please don't waste his time."

But Jack insisted. Supposing it was something worse? And, it was more than likely that the same thing had happened to Alice. By the second day she would be on her feet again and able to get a message to him.

"I'll go round tonight," Marg said to Jack on Tuesday, when he was still unable to get an answer. He had tried the Powells' home number but they would be at work themselves. Derek would be out on the road and he did not know where Liz worked these days.

"Marg, this might sound a bit over the top, but those phone calls and things, you don't suppose, well . . ."

"Don't even say it, Vera. Don't tempt fate. Besides, that's all in the past." But the same thing had crossed her own mind but only because Alice was so reliable. Surely she would have found a way to get in touch before now.

Later that evening Marg puffed up the hill from the town and found Alice's flat quite easily. She had been there before, as had Vera, when Alice had a moving-in party, and once Marg had been somewhere she never forgot the way. Pausing in the hall to get her breath she glanced at the letters on the table. One was addressed to Alice. It had Saturday's date and was posted locally, which suggested Alice had not been downstairs yesterday. She picked it up, she might as well deliver it personally. It was a brown envelope which could only be a bill. She knocked on the door and waited, anticipating Alice opening it, clad in nightdress and dressing gown. A minute later she knocked again, louder this time, then put her ear against the door, not caring if anyone saw her. She was more than worried now. No sounds came from within. Marg hesitated. What was the girl's name, the one who lived downstairs? Rosie? No, Josie. She plodded down, her footsteps heavy, the boards creaking beneath her weight, and replaced the letter on the table. There were two doors on the ground floor. She tried both and got a response from the second. "Oh," she said, taking in the bizarrely dressed young woman. "Are you Alice's friend?"

"I'm Josie, yes."

"Good. I need to get in touch with her, do you know where she is?"

Josie's mind worked quickly. Alice had been having those calls and letters. True, it seemed to have stopped, but could this woman be somehow responsible? And if she needed to get hold of Alice urgently, why not telephone? "No, I don't."

"When did you last see her?"

"Don't think me rude, but I really don't see that it's any of your business."

"I'm sorry. I'm Mrs Finch, Marg Finch. Alice may have mentioned me." Josie did not respond. "Look, this really

151

is important. She hasn't been to work, we're worried about her."

"I still can't help you, Mrs Finch. I've no idea where she is."

"All right. Thanks." Marg had to leave it at that.

Josie put it out of her mind.

Random thoughts passed through Alice's mind. Work, her parents, James, her future – if she had one, that is – and her own stupidity for allowing herself to be in this position, for not having been insistent he let her go. It was crazy, but how was anyone supposed to be prepared for such a thing?

Gradually her heartbeat had regulated itself and she was able to think more calmly. There had to be a way out of this, it was just that she couldn't see it for the moment. An overwhelming feeling of tiredness came over her and all she wanted to do was sleep. But that must not happen. How much more vulnerable she would be if she did.

She did not know if James had slept. When she had come down on Sunday morning the other bedroom door had been wide open, the bed neatly made. Perhaps he had dozed in the chair.

Now, when he spoke, the words seemed not to be directed at her but at some unseen person. But each time she moved he was on his feet, next to her. Finally, she leant forward over the table and closed her eyes but sleep was impossible.

"I need the lavatory, James," she said. She had checked on a previous visit. There was no escape that way. The window had another security lock, the door itself had no lock at all. If she smashed the glass James would be through the door before she even had a foot on the windowsill.

They were miles from anywhere, the church spire she could see was way in the distance and even supposing she got out of the cottage it was unlikely she would get far on foot before he caught up with her. Hunger and lack of a proper night's sleep had left her weak.

One thing was certain, none of the keys were hidden in the bathroom. Very quietly she slid back the door of the cabinet over the sink. It was empty. Nor were they in the low toilet cistern. The car keys were of secondary importance if she could not get out of the cottage. There would be no hesitation in driving it now. She tried to rationalise the situation. Surely her mother, knowing about the letters, would start worrying again if she did not hear from her over the weekend or if she continually got no answer from her own telephone. Why hadn't she said James had a surprise for her? Because Liz did not seem interested, because, for some reason, Liz did not like James. No, that wasn't true. She knew her mother well enough to recognise when she disliked someone. She had been pleasant and friendly to him; it was his relationship with her that Liz didn't like, not the man himself. And Liz was wise enough to make no comment knowing Alice would make up her own mind whatever she thought.

The hours ticked slowly by. It was almost midday. It should have been lovely, miles away from anywhere, plenty of food and wine, the sun shining in a clear sky, and it had turned into this.

Twice she jumped, when James shouted, ranting and raving about some girl in the car, about having control, about Larry. None of it made any sense to her.

"He saw you," James said at one point, addressing her directly. "Larry saw you."

"Why did you do it, James? Why did you make those calls?"

"I didn't make any calls. Not me, Alice, I wouldn't hurt you."

"You are, by keeping me here. I want to go home."

"You did it Alice, you'll pay. You shouldn't have made me like you. I warned you. You have to learn to treat men properly. I know you can, Alice. Keith," he said with venom. Later, when he was quieter he said in such a normal voice that she thought the whole thing had been a dream "I don't want to hurt you, Alice. Larry might, but I won't." The voice might have been normal; the words were not.

She had no idea how to react to his moods which fluctuated between a sneering, callous dominance to introspective mutterings. Each passing hour when he did not touch her renewed her hope she would come out of it safely. She tried to keep him talking and when she failed, encouraged him to drink. It occurred to her to scream, scream long and loud, not that anyone would hear but it might bring James round to some semblance of normality. On the other hand it might send him over the top. All the time her mind was working yet no solution came to her.

At last Alice could stand it no longer. When he went out to the kitchen she picked up a chair and threw it at the window. A small pane cracked, then there was silence. Pain shot up her arm as James grabbed her from behind. He smiled, but it was a twist of the mouth. "Take off your tights," he said.

"What?"

154

"You heard."

Her head snapped to one side as he hit her across the face. What she had dreaded was about to happen. She stepped out of her shoes and turned her back, sensing the strength his anger was giving him. She choked down a small, defeatist sob, she would not let him see her vulnerability.

"Give them to me."

She passed him her tights, holding the shape of her body after the hours she had been wearing them. James grabbed both her wrists and wrapped the stretchy material tightly around them, pulling it until it was painful, then tied a knot.

"Please," she whispered. "Please don't." She pulled away, struggling with her bonds, the knots of which only became tighter. She should have seen it coming and struggled with the man himself. James stepped towards her and roughly pushed her onto the settee. A spring creaked beneath her as she tried to keep upright. It took her several seconds to realise James was no longer in the room. She heard a crash from the kitchen followed by cursing. When he returned he was holding a ball of string, the sort used to wrap parcels. He cut off a long length and doubled it before securing her ankles together. The string was rough, if she moved too much if chaffed, but that was not important. Her legs were tied together, he was not going to rape her. It no longer mattered what he wanted from her or why she was there, all that concerned her was getting away.

Alice closed her eyes and went back over the past two days. It was her own fault, there must have been many ways she could have escaped while she was still able to move around. She had believed that although

James had issued those threats he would be incapable of holding her prisoner longer than the weekend. That kind of thing happened to other people, not women like Alice Powell.

The sun moved a few degrees westward and shone through the front window. Outside birds twittered but she cursed them as she tried to listen for the sound of traffic. It was difficult to estimate how far off the road they were as James had had to take the lane very slowly. But the road was a minor one with little traffic on it on Saturday.

The place is furnished, she thought, maybe he's only renting it, maybe the previous occupants haven't been gone long. In which case there might be some post. To deliver out here the postman would need at least a bike, if not a van. When he approached the door she would have a clear view of him through the window and she would scream until she had no breath left. Hours of darkness ticked slowly by.

In the morning she stared at the path. No one came.

"I went round there, Jack," Marg said. "She defintitely wasn't there. Have you tried her parents?"

"I couldn't get any answer yesterday, or this morning. And I don't know where Liz works." Jack took out a small cigar and lit it. Already he had smoked his day's ration. "I'll try and get hold of her this evening."

"I think we ought to tell the police. They know about the phone calls and letters, they'll take it seriously."

"We can't, not until her parents know. And there's always the possibility they know where she is."

Marg was doubtful. From the few occasions she had met Liz Powell she recognised a responsible woman

156

who would inform her daughter's employer if Alice wasn't coming to work. She also knew Alice would not disappear leaving everyone to worry.

"Look, Marg, I'll keep trying to the end of the day and if there's no joy I'll go round to see the Powells, then it's up to them to contact the police."

Marg went back to her packing but she wasn't satisfied. It was unlike Jack to be hesitant over what he knew he ought to do. She looked back and saw him pick up the telephone receiver.

"I don't like it," she told Vera. "It's all wrong. Jack knows more than he's telling us."

"Oh, my God."

"What?"

"Alice, she's been going out with his son."

"With James? Don't be daft, girl, I'd've known."

But for once Vera was one up on Marg. "She told me on Thursday evening, when she came round to see me. With Greg worrying over me and coming back to work, I completely forgot." She was being kind to Marg, she would not have broken her promise to Alice.

"Why the secret?" Marg was hurt, but in a way she could understand Alice's reticence. The other women would have teased her mercilessly.

"Perhaps they've eloped," Stella offered, and received two distainful glanes for her efforts.

Jack rang Ruth who confirmed James was not yet home. Please don't let anything have happened to her, he thought as he redialled the Powells' number on the off chance one of them had some time off.

At six he got an answer. Liz Powell picked up the telephone and cheerfully said the number. "Liz, it's me. Jack."

157

"Jack?" For a second or two there was silence but he had heard her indrawn breath as she said his name.

"I wouldn't bother you at home, but look, we've got a problem."

"What's going on, Jack?"

How could he tell her over the phone? If Alice was there she would have said so. "I need to talk to you urgently. Could you meet me somewhere?"

"If you think you can . . ."

"No, Liz. Please. This is important."

"All right. Where?"

"The Three Tuns?"

"OK. I'll be there in about fifteen minutes." She replaced the receiver. The Three Tuns was on the outskirts of the town, not the sort of place she imagined Jack frequented. Liz left a note for Derek and went out to the car. Only when she turned the ignition did it dawn on her. Alice. It had to be Alice, who had not answered her phone on Sunday or last night. Alice had found out and was avoiding her, might never even speak to her again. A lump came into Liz's throat. What would she do if she lost the friendship and love of her daughter, her favourite child? For the first time she admitted it. Mothers were supposed to favour their sons but although she loved him, Mark had always been independent, brushing off any affection, almost embarrassed by it. He was the same with Nicola, but she seemed not to mind.

If Alice knew, then so did James and that was what Jack wanted to talk to her about. Her worst fears had come true. She must now face them. She forced herself to drive within the speed limit and reached the pub exactly fifteen minutes after she left the house.

158

Jack was at the bar, half facing the door. "Liz, thanks for coming. Gin and bitter lemon?"

She smiled ruefully. He had not forgotten what she drank.

They took their drinks to a table. "I don't know where to start, and it all might be a storm in a teacup but I couldn't say it over the phone."

"Jack, get on with it."

"Yes. Look, Liz, do you know where Alice is?"

"Right now? No."

"She didn't come in to work yesterday or today."

"She must be ill, she wouldn't take time off." But Liz was trying not to think of the alternatives. Alice wasn't ill, she would have answered the telephone on one of the occasions she rang, because she would not necessarily know who was calling.

"Marjorie Finch went to the flat. Alice wasn't there."

Liz's hand went up to her throat in an automatically defensive gesture. What was Jack saying, that Alice couldn't even bear to be anywhere near her?

"You know, I take it, that she's been seeing James?"

"Yes," Liz answered quietly.

"Did you say anything?"

Liz shook her head and her dark hair swung and Jack smelled the perfume she had always worn.

"Nor did I. I couldn't. I thought it would fizzle out."

"So neither of them know? Oh, God, Jack, in that case . . ."

Jack rested a hand over hers. It was a gesture of comfort, nothing more. "You don't need me to tell you Alice wouldn't go away without letting someone know. I think we'll have to go to the police."

"Those phone calls, and the letters. I was worried sick

159

but I thought it was some crank, you know, someone who was afraid of women face to face. It's my fault, I should've . . ."

"Liz, take it easy." He gave her his handkerchief. "Drink your drink. It's not so much I think she's in danger, it's just the consequences. James is missing too."

She looked up and stared into his face with horror. "You mean they've run off together?"

"I'm not sure. But it's a possibility," Jack admitted, heavily.

"It's our fault," Liz exclaimed. "If we hadn't done what we did this would not have mattered."

"I know. But I don't regret it. We needed each other at the time."

"That's all very well, Jack. We made a mistake and, fortunately, no one got hurt. Not then, but they might now. And it doesn't alter the fact that my daughter is possibly having an affair with her half-brother." There was no doubt that Alice was Jack's child and she had hated herself for letting Derek believe she had been premature. He had never questioned her, never had a moment's doubt, as Alice had been tiny. "You may not think she's in any danger but I'm going to the police anyway. If she doesn't know about us she's no reason not to say where she is." Liz stood up.

"I'll come with you," Jack said. "Do you want to let Derek know?"

She paused, unsure of how much the police would need to know. "Not just yet. And Ruth?"

He smiled, grimly. "No, not just yet."

They took both cars as they would, presumably, be going their separate ways afterwards. "There's a slim chance they're not together. James told us he was going

160

to visit friends in Wiltshire. We can't check because we don't know who they are."

Liz unlocked her car door. "He's never had a job, has he?"

"No."

They drove off, Jack leading, Liz grew more and more worried. She'd known, somehow, that James had lied about himself when he'd come to lunch.

"It's very good of you," Marg said when she returned from her brief conversation with Josie, to discover Mr Green had started the meal. The potatoes were turned down low and he had opened a tin of peas. He was unsure of what to do with the liver, but a couple of onions were sliced, ready, on the chopping board.

Marg rinsed the liver and cut it into pieces of the same size. It would only take a minute. "She wasn't there. And her neighbour wasn't exactly helpful."

"Mightn't it be best to leave it to someone else?" Mr Green knew she was upset but he couldn't see the point in getting involved in other people's affairs, not when there were others closer to home to help.

Marg swung around. "She's my friend. I care what happens to her. She'd do the same for me."

"Nothing may have happened," he said quietly, sorry to have offended her but knowing she had a tendency to over-react, apart from an inherent nosiness. Except, in this instance he saw her concern was genuine. "But if it's bothering you that much, why don't you go to the police?"

"You're right. I'm sorry, I shouldn't have shouted. Jack's been trying to contact her parents since Monday. If he hasn't got hold of them by tonight he said he'd go to the police. They can't be out three nights in a row, surely?" And she was thinking if Jack had real doubts about Alice's safety he'd've have waited on the front doorstep until they returned. But Marg did not know the difficulties that might create.

She fried the liver and dished up, no longer afraid to discuss things with Mr Green because he had shown himself to be a true comfort. She cheered herself up with the thought that Alice, on a whim, had fancied a few days to herself. But deep down she knew this was not so.

Phyllis found a new job very quickly, realising how very lucky she was. Usually, if you were over forty, there was little chance of being taken on. Firms wanted younger staff these days. She had had to settle for a drop in salary, but had agreed to start as a secretary for a firm of solicitors the following Monday. Meanwhile, she had had to go back and face Jack Winter, to ask for the necessary documentation her new employers required. Now her life had taken a new turn she felt mean at having walked out on a kind and generous employer.

Jack, however, was distracted and did not seem to have taken offence at her actions.

Phyllis thanked him and started to offer an apology.

"It doesn't matter, Phyllis. The new girl, Mandy's coping. And good luck."

Downstairs several of the women clustered around her, eager to hear her reasons for leaving and to pick up any potential gossip. It turned out to be the other way around. It was Phyllis who learned that Alice seemed to have disappeared.

She strolled home, unaware of the true facts of the matter, not connecting this piece of news with her suspicions that James Winter, whom she knew had once gone through her personnel records, might be the man responsible for frightening the women with telephone calls and letters.

To her shame, she knew she had not mentioned it to Jack in case he accused her of lack of security. On the other hand, James was his son and often boasted he would one day take over the whole thing. Was it so bad, then, that he had abused her absence from the room on that occasion?

Chapter Eight

He carried her as far as the bathroom door and dumped her on the floor while he opened it. With difficulty he untied the knots around her ankles. Alice held out her wrists but James shook his head. Tears of shame filled her eyes. How was she to manage without assistance from him. The complete subjugation was humiliating enough; to have him stand there was total abasement. And yet although his eyes were on her he was looking through her. He no longer spoke to her, his words were aimed at someone else, someone inside his head.

"James, please untie my hands. I won't try to get away, I promise."

He smiled as he slapped her again.

"Why are you doing this?" she asked quietly when she was back on the settee. "If I knew I could help you."

"The other one said that."

She waited. Here was a moment of lucidity.

"That he could help. Larry did." He held his head. "No, I did."

God help me, she thought, he's mad. But she had to know the answer. "You're Larry, aren't you?"

"Who did you think I was?"

"James Winter."

"He's the other one, he doesn't know anything."

"James . . ."

"Don't call me that."

Alice flinched as he lunged forward, waiting for the blow, but he took a deep breath and stood straight.

Alice lay on her side with her knees bent. James had immediately replaced the string when she had finished in the bathroom. Every muscle ached but the hunger had worn off. James had remained in the chair throughout Monday night and she had tried to sleep through her discomfort. His drinking was spasmodic, nothing for several hours then he would take it straight from the bottle. The wine could not last for ever, neither could the food, not that he was eating anything, but there would have to come a point when he needed to leave. What then? If she was bound and locked in with no telephone what chance did she have? And if he didn't come back? She would starve to death.

Something kept her going, something told her some-one would realise something was wrong. The recurring thought came back. If James had squared it with Jack he would not be missing her. If her mother was worried Jack would tell her she was away for a week, or a fortnight, and although Liz would find it hard to swallow, she would accept what Jack said.

"I'm thirsty."

James had his head to one side as if he was listening to something. Alice listened too, in case it was a car, then realised whatever voices he was hearing would not reach her ears. "Larry, I need a drink." It came out firmly, as if she was the one in control and surprisingly it worked. She would bite the glass, break it, make her mouth bleed, then surely he would do something. Or keep it in her mouth and hurt him with it.

165

But the water was in a thick, porcelain mug. It was lukewarm, from the hot tap. He held it at an angle and some splashed down her clothes and felt like ice against her skin. Alice realised she was becoming ill. Her joints were on fire, her head ached and, as she had only needed the toilet on three occasions, she guessed she was becoming dehydrated. There were also moments when she lost track of time. She was not even sure it was Tuesday. There was no clock in the room and she could not see her watch which was hidden beneath the tights and was cutting into her wrist.

Hours must have passed because the sun had moved from one side of the window to the other and was beginning to set. She did not think she could survive another night.

Later, when James slept, she allowed herself some self-pity. Tears ran down her cheeks but she made herself stop. There was no means of blowing her nose. For half an hour she sniffed then, able to bear it no longer, picked up the scatter cushion with both hands and used it to wipe her nose. If she was to be treated like an animal she might as well behave like one. Exhaustion overcame her and she slept solidly for two hours.

"We'll eat now," James said unexpectedly. Alice opened her eyes. He was standing over her. It was still dark. The time of day was unimportant, she needed food. Bitterly she regretted turning down the offer of breakfast on Sunday morning; in that other lifetime. Her skin felt cold but there was nothing to cover herself with, nothing sharp in the room to free herself with, nothing she could do but wait. She smelled burning and her heart thumped as she imagined James setting fire to the place and leaving her in it.

Saliva filled her mouth when the aroma of frying onions reached her. Whatever he served up she would eat. Slowly, she reminded herself, because she had been so long without anything. Earlier thoughts of refusing all nourishment had disappeared. That may work with someone rational but James was way beyond reasoned thinking.

She had once read about a hostage, a man who had been kept for years in far inferior conditions to her own. He had said that although the guards beat him there were moments of kindness and after his release he felt ashamed for being grateful for what were really every day human courtesies. But those moments had kept him going, given him hope that he would survive and, despite everything a bond had formed between himself and the hostage-takers. It was inevitable, he claimed, that when there was no one else with whom to converse, and after long periods of isolation, any form of communication was welcome. Alice did not agree. Whatever she had felt for James had disappeared. Emotion of some description was required to form a bond, even hate. She did not hate him, he no longer existed as a man. She did not allow herself to think that the man she read of had been held captive for years, that after a while she, too, might feel as he had done.

For a second she thought it had all been a cruel joke. James carried a plate towards her, his face relaxed, smiling, as when she had first met him. He put the plate on a small table and waited until she had got herself into a sitting position. Any minute now he would untie her, apologise, tell her he had had a brain storm. Anything. She would believe him, go along with it and be free.

But he did not untie her. He continued smiling and took a sip from the glass of wine she had assumed was meant for herself. When he picked up the fork she saw the food had been roughly cut up. He was going to feed her. So be it, she must eat. In the darkness relieved only by the light from a three quarter moon, she could not make out what the meal consisted of. Onions, yes, and some sort of pale meat. She took the first forkful with her teeth and began to chew, gagging as she realised it was chicken, raw in the centre. She had to spit it out without offending him. Raising both hands she got rid of it. "I'm sorry, it's not quite cooked, James."

"Larry," he screamed and punched her on the side of the head. Flinging an arm out he swiped the plate to the floor. She was not even able to eat the onions. Straightening slowly he began to chuckle. The sound frightened her more than the violence. "Oh, yes," he said, "I think I'll do that."

He sat down on the edge of the armchair and swigged from a bottle of wine. "I'll tell her all about James, shall I? We go back a long way, don't we?"

He was unshaven and dirty. As Alice watched him she realised the last links with sanity had snapped.

"Yes," Detective Inspector Pearson said, "it's already on file." He studied the parents. Not married; to each other, that is, but both without their respective partner. Alice Powell and James Winter were both of an age when they could please themselves, they were under no obligation, other than common courtesy to tell anyone of their whereabouts as long as they had not committed a crime, but he could not brush aside the fact of the letters, which were in the file, and the telephone calls. There was just a possibility their anxiety was justified, and if he ignored the possibility of foul play and something really was a miss, it would be the end of his career, or, certainly of the chance of promotion. The more obvious explanation, as both full sets of parents were not present, was that they had done a bunk because of parental disaproval. Jack Winter was a prominent figure in the town, maybe he, or his wife, expected better for their son than one of the factory hands. Yet Elizabeth Powell came across as well educated, caring and down to earth and if her daughter took after her in those respects, let alone the looks department, he could see no reason for any objections.

"When were either of them last seen? We'll start with you, Mr Winter."

"Saturday morning. We were having breakfast and James came into the kitchen for coffee. He had already forewarned us he was going away for the weekend, to stay with friends in Wiltshire. As I said, my wife and I had no idea who they might be but there was no reason to disbelieve him."

"In which case that's where he might be." It was not a question because he was thinking if it *was* so it made the chances of Alice Powell being in danger, or worse, even greater. "Mrs Powell?"

"I haven't seen Alice since Friday night. She called in briefly and said James was going to pick her or from the flat at eight-thirty. I tried telephoning several times over the weekend, and again on Monday evening, but there was no reply."

"But you weren't concerned then?"

"I had no reason to be. Alice has her own place and her own life. We keep in touch throughout the week and I just assumed she was out enjoying herself." Pearson had made her feel as if she was not a caring mother and she resented it.

169

Jack sensed Liz's anger and knew it would not help. He diffused it by saying, "A member of my staff, Mrs Marjorie Finch, went round to Alice's flat on Tuesday but she wasn't in. We were concerned about her at work. As Mrs Powell said, Alice has always been reliable."

"All right, we'll try the hospital first." DI Pearson realised by their expressions they had not thought of that.

"No. Alice carried enough identification with her, and I'm sure James does too. It's four days, someone would've got in touch if they were badly injured."

"Mrs Powell, let me be the judge of how things are done."

Liz blushed. He was right but she was in need of greater action, she wanted every police officer in the British Isles out there looking for her daughter.

It was almost two hours before they left, having provided lists of everyone Alice and James knew, the registration number of James's car and Alice's address in case a neighbour had seen her at a time later than Friday evening.

"What now, Jack?"

"We do as he said. We go home and wait. Best to be near the telephone in case there's any news."

Neither cared now if their secret was discovered, all that mattered was that Alice was safe. For some reason Jack did not think his son was in any danger.

"Where the hell have you been? I was worried sick."

"Didn't you see my note?" Liz was tired, worn out with the anxiety of knowing Alice was going out with James, and now this. She wanted to be able to close her mind, to stop thinking of all the ifs.

"I saw it. I wouldn't call three hours popping out for a few minutes."

"Derek, come and sit down. I need to talk to you."

He followed her into the living-room, puzzled, but not particularly worried.

"Pour me a drink, would you. A large one."

Derek handed her the glass and thought he had better have one himself if she needed that much fortification.

"It's Alice. You know she's been seeing James Winter."

"Yes."

"They've both disappeared."

"They've what?"

"Alice hasn't been to work this week." She went on to tell him the rest of it but omitted the fact that the girl he believed to be his daughter was with her half-brother. Derek was pale, his hands shaking by the time she had finished.

"What are the police doing about it?" he asked.

"I don't think they took us seriously at first, but because of the other matter – the nasty notes and phone calls – they are looking for them," Liz replied, wearily.

"There must be something more we can do," Derek exclaimed. "I know Alice, she wouldn't put us through this. Something must be very wrong."

But there was nothing to do but wait.

"Get round to the Wentons," DI Pearson said. "The lad made a nuisance of himself when the engagement was broken off." That piece of information was also in the file. If the Winter boy *was* off la-di-da-ing it on some country estate it could be that Keith Wenton had used

171

the chance to get his woman back, even if his methods were a little unorthodox.

Meanwhile, he'd get the nearest patrol car to have a chat with Alice's neighbours. He wasn't going to make too big a deal out of it but he was certainly going to go through the motions.

Then he thought about it. All right, parents were often mistaken about their offspring, but both Alice's mother and her employer said the same thing. Perhaps he'd better have a word with the Chief.

An hour later PC Collins reported in from his panda car that Alice Powell had last been seen by her friend and neighbour, Josie Evans, on Friday after work when she had rushed out of the door saying she was going to her mother's. "She thinks she heard her come in, sir, about eleven, but she can't be certain because she didn't know who else was out at the time." The other residents had not seen her since the previous day.

DI Pearson, on the Chief's orders, had made sure the registration number of James Winter's car had been circulated to traffic division. With a bit of luck someone would pick him, or both of them, up.

Joan Wenton gave a sniff of disapproval when the man on her doorstep introduced himself. "What now?"

Detective Constable Monroe was taken aback. The name Wenton meant nothing to him but the woman was acting if a call from the police was a regular occurrence.

"Mrs Wenton?"

"Yes."

"Is Keith Wenton at home?"

"Why?"

"I'd like to ask him a couple of questions."

"What about?"

DC Monroe took a deep breath. Public relations were one thing, obstruction was another. "If it's any easier I can get a patrol car to pick him up and take him down to the station." Not strictly true but it did the trick.

"You'd better come in. Keith!" she called up the stairs. He had stayed in all evening and was up in his room either listening to music or watching sport on the portable television purchased for that reason. It was quarter to ten. He would not be in bed yet.

Keith's shocked reaction to the news seemed genuine enough, but, if guilty, he would have prepared himself for questioning. However, he had taken Jackie Pearce out on Friday night, worked on Saturday morning which the electricity board would confirm, gone to a football match with two friends in the afternoon and gone to the cinema with Jackie on Saturday evening.

"And Sunday?" DC Monroe persisted.

"You really don't think this is anything to do with me, do you?" Keith asked, frustratedly.

"We have to check."

Keith saw the logic. He had been a pain pestering Alice like that, and they had his name on record because of the phone call business. "I played football on Sunday morning."

"Belong to the Bell Street club, do you?"

"Yes. Why?"

"My son's in the under-eights side. Anyway, you were saying?"

"Came home for dinner and stayed in Sunday after-noon. Back to work on Monday."

173

All that Keith Wenton had told him could, and would, be checked but DC Monroe had already ruled him out.

"I always said that girl was trouble," Joan Wenton commented when they were alone. She was totally unprepared for the reaction.

"How dare you! Jesus, you make me sick. You did everything in your power to persuade her to come back to me. Don't you ever think of anyone but yourself? I know we're not together any more but I still care about Alice. Something dreadful might've happened. And what about her parents?"

"Keith, I —"

"I haven't finished!" It was time all this was said. "Ever since Dad died you've been totally selfish. You've tried to keep me tied to your apron strings and you wanted Alice that way too. She was lucky, she escaped!"

"Oh!" Joan sank into into a chair. "I feel dizzy, Keith. Get me my tablets, there's a dear."

"Sod your bloody tablets!" A bright flush spread up from Joan's neck. Keith had never sworn in her presence. "There isn't anything wrong with you, don't you understand that? I don't know why that doctor prescribes them, they're probably placebos anyway. You don't need then, you use them as a means of getting pity. Well, it doesn't work any more."

"Keith?" But he had flung himself from the room and run upstairs. Joan jumped up but it was too late. She heard the gurgle of water as the toilet cistern refilled. "My tablets!" she cried.

Keith came back down slowly not knowing if he had done the right thing but all he could think of was what Alice might be going through. The police would not be making inquiries if she had simply taken a few days off work.

Joan was staring rigidly ahead of her. He saw he would have to be the first to speak. "Mum, you could do so much more with your life." He hesitated, then, realising how far he had gone, thought he might as well say it all. "You could go out and meet people, get your hair done or something."

"My hair?" She touched it. She had no idea that he noticed such things. She was his mother, she thought he accepted her just as she was.

"Think about it. Make a new start, it's not too late."

"Where are you going?"

"I'm going over to the Powells' to see if there's anything I can do."

"But it's ten o'clock." Even as she spoke she realised how ridiculously conventional she sounded. If it was three a.m. Liz and Derek would not be asleep.

By Thursday, everyone at Winter's Confectionery Company realised how serious the situation was when they heard an appeal on local radio for Alice or James to come forward. Jack Winter had not been seen since Tuesday and Mandy was taking his calls.

"I keep thinking the worst," Vera admitted, biting most of her puce lipstick off in agitation. "Alice wouldn't do anything stupid; something's happened to her."

"She's tough," Marg reassured her. "If there's any way out of whatever she's got into, she'll find it." But Marg's heart wasn't in it. She had put two and two together. It wasn't just Jack and Phyllis who spent time in the office where the personnel files were kept. Now she thought of it, James Winter did too. Whoever sent those letters was not normal. If it was James and he was with Alice, it was more than possible he would carry out those threats. Ought she to contact Jack and tell him what she suspected? Jack had enough on his plate as it was. And she could well be very wrong about James's guilt. Besides, the police were looking for them anyway, now.

Against her better judgment she decided to keep quiet.

Alice was no longer afraid. She had gone past feeling anything; her brain was as numb as her limbs. There was a red ridge appearing around her ankles. She looked at it with fascination. Sometimes, because the functioning part of her mind told her she should, she wriggled her toes and fingers. The wine had run out. James was drinking whisky, but not at the same rate. There had been no more food but she forced herself to ask for water, always remembering to call him Larry. Even so, her tongue felt furred and she was experiencing a stinging sensation which was probably cystitis. If only he would talk to me, she thought, unaware that two days ago it was the last thing she wanted. The idea of being rescued was forgotten, it was just a case of how long she could last. Even if James left for more drink supplies, Alice knew she did not possess the strength to move from the settee. She didn't even want to. It had become her place and she was content to lie there for ever. Every item in the room was as familar to her as if she had spent her whole life in it.

James was in as bad a state. He looked ill, his face blotchy, dark shadows under his eyes, and he could only lumber when he walked. Sometimes he muttered, sometimes he shouted, none of it affected Alice. It had become the norm. The next time she asked for a drink she had to shout herself, not that it was very loud, her voice seemed to be going. "Larry!" On the sixth time he responded. "Water!"

"Water." The simple instruction seemed to take ages to sink in but he brought back the mug, half full. It was as if for each of them forming the most ordinary, every-day words and actions had become feats of enormous proportions.

James knew on the Saturday that he wasn't safe, that even here Larry was with him, and by Sunday that he was taking over. He had tried to prevent it, tried desperately hard to keep him away from Alice but Larry had reminded him it was his idea in the first place.

Alice had changed, James saw that soon after their arrival. She was wary of him, unsettled, as if she wanted to leave immediately, and after all his efforts he could not allow that to happen. He needed time to persuade her they were right for each other. But now James was no longer in control. Larry, as always, was dominant, Larry had known that the only way Alice was going to stay was if she was made to. But James had forgotten all that. All he knew now was that she was here, with him, lying comfortably on the settee, smiling at him and saying nice things; or so Larry was telling him.

Sometimes he was confused, when the voice, James's voice, told him not to drink, but James was a fool who had never done anything in life.

He smiled at Alice and tried to work out what she was saying. "Water." She wanted a drink. He had told her he was going to spoil her, to treat her like

177

a princess. If she wanted water, of course he would get it for her.

Jack had not rung Ruth to tell her he would be late. She was just beginning to wonder where he was when she heard the car in the drive.

On Tuesday night after he and Liz had left the police station he had had no idea what he would say to his wife or how she would take it. Her pale, lightly freckled face was beautiful even in repose. She looked at him steadily, her eyes a clear green, and knew instinctively he was ready to tell her.

She sat beside him and held his hand. "Do you want a drink? I'll join you," she added hastily, seeing him hesitate.

Their glasses were on the coffee table. Ruth left hers untouched. "It's James and Alice, isn't it?"

Jack nodded and began to explain. Ruth put two fingers over his lips. "I've been doing a lot of thinking, Jack. He's never been like the others, has he? It's our fault, we've turned a blind eye."

"What do you mean?"

"I was remembering his tantrums when he was little, how he fought and screamed when he couldn't get his own way. I don't think he's ever grown out of it."

"What're you saying, Ruthie?"

"He's unbalanced, Jack."

She was right and he knew it, but the last thing he expected was to hear such an admission from her.

"I'm afraid he might harm her and I don't know what that would do to us."

"To us?"

"You wouldn't be able to live with it, Jack. I know you too well. I know what you feel for Alice."

"Ruth, I . . ."

"Let me finish." Ruth took a sip of her drink and wet her lips. "When the children were born I didn't cope very well. I suppose nowadays it would be recognised as postnatal depression, but it was worse with James. I realise it wasn't all down to me, he was a difficult baby, but it took me longer to get over it that time than with Polly or Simon." Ruth paused, recalling how she had let herself go. That, alone, would not have bothered Jack, but she had become withdrawn, miserable and tearful. Unable to bear herself as she was she had turned away from Jack. "You see, it's bad enough that James may have done something wrong. You'd find that hard enough to cope with, but it's because Alice is involved as well." Ruth looked down at her hands which were clasped in her lap. "I know, Jack. I knew you were having an affair at the time but believe me, it didn't seem to matter, I didn't really care about anything. It was only later, when I overheard you talking to Liz about how you'd give Alice a job and look after her that I realised all of it. Alice is your child, isn't she?"

"Oh, Ruth." Jack Winter bowed his head and, for the first time, his wife saw him cry. She did not touch him, it would humiliate him further. Instead she finished her drink and left the room. She neither wanted nor needed explanations or apologies; it was a relief it was out in the open. She had coped with the knowledge alone all these years. Now it was Jack's turn. Ruth Winter was astonished at the sense of power she felt, but she must never let it show.

In the modern, well-equiped kitchen, she flattened

179

some veal, dipped it in egg and breadcrumbs and put it in a pan with butter. It was time both of them ate a proper meal. Like Jack, she had no fears for her son's safety and although she was concerned about Alice, she was not her own daughter. Ruth Winter suddenly recognised her own strength of character.

There was no immediate response to the radio appeal. On Friday the police began to dig deeper; speaking to people who knew James and Alice, looking into their backgrounds.

Ruth calmly answered questions, withholding nothing. It was her turn to be in control and she had found the strength for it. "If you're asking if he's had any psychiatric treatment, then the answer is no, but he's not gregarious and his concentration span is poor." As a child she recalled him having an imaginary friend, one whose name he would not reveal. That was normal for an eight-year-old boy but with James it had lasted until he was thirteen. She did not know the imaginary friend still existed.

"Mrs Winter, do you own any other properties, places where your son might have gone?" DC Monroe questioned.

Ruth shook her head. It was Jack who spoke as he entered the room. He had not been dressed when the detective arrived at eight-fifteen and he refused to speak to him from a position of disadvantage. "I may be wealthy, but I've never seen the point of owning more than one house. You can't live in two places at once."

"And your son's financial position?"

"He doesn't have any real money of his own, only what we give him. The rest is in trust until he's thirty."

"All right. Is there anywhere he particularly likes?"

"I don't understand you."

"Places he enjoyed on holiday as a kid, places with happy memories, that sort of thing?" He asked the question because the more they learned of Alice Powell the more they realised she was probably being held against her will.

"None that I can recall. Ruth?"

"I don't think so." Now she thought about it there did not seem to be anything that fired James with enthusiasm.

"Well?" DI Pearson said sharply when DC Monroe returned from the Winters'.

"Nothing doing. Nothing from traffic I take it? It's not looking good, Sir, is it?"

Pearson did not answer. He was annoyed with himself for having made further inquiries about those letters. If they're of any relevance, he reminded himself. He opened the file again. "Go back to the Winters, see if they recognise the writing." He handed Monroe photocopies of the originals.

Only when Liz Powell saw Keith did she burst into tears. It was a reminder of what might have been. But it was useless thinking that way. If Alice had gone ahead with the marriage she would have ended up miserable, perhaps more miserable than she was at that moment, because she had to hope they were wrong.

"I don't know what to say, Liz." Keith put an arm around her.

"I know." She wiped her eyes. They were smaller without liner and mascara. "But it was thoughtful of

181

you to come. I'll make some tea." Tea, she thought, the British panacea. But it was something to do.

Keith stayed for an hour but he had to get up early for work the following morning. "I'll come back again," he said when he left.

He waited until Friday, imagining Alice would be safely home by then. He was wrong. In the kitchen Liz tried to make conversation but he saw it was a struggle, that she wanted to be alone. Derek remained in the living room. It seemed they could not bear to even talk to each other.

Liz had finally given in and not gone to work. Her boss had insisted upon it for compassionate reasons but also because she was giving out the wrong change. She was also finding the consolatory remarks of the customers who knew her more than she could bear, and had snapped at a regular customer who had assured her everything would be all right.

Derek, too, had taken time off but wondered why. He and Liz seemed to have nothing to say to one another. He looked up as she came to sit beside him. "I don't know how I can get through another day," she said. "I just want to know." What she meant was that it would be easier to cope with positive information, even if it was that Alice was dead.

Mark had called in every day but had the sense not to bring baby Damien. He, too, had been questioned but had not seen his sister since they had all had Sunday lunch together.

James's siblings had received a visit from their respective local police and had not heard from him either, not even by telephone. Typically, Polly offered to drop everything and come home, but Ruth would not allow it. Besides, she needed time alone with Jack to enable him to come to terms with her knowledge of his affair and daughter. He was still unable to look her in the eye. Polly would be an added complication.

For some reason, as time went on, Ruth began to think that James would not hurt Alice. There was no question of it being a kidnap where money was an issue, of course. James received an adequate allowance and would only have to ask in an emergency. Anyway, the Powells were not in a position to have much spare. She assumed therefore that James wanted Alice, but the feeling was not reciprocated so he had simply taken what he wanted. Of all her children, James had been closest to her because he was quiet and remained dependent on her for longer. Now, with a jolt of surprise, she realised she did not like him very much.

"Have we produced some sort of monster?" she asked, not expecting an answer, after they had identified their son's writing. The notes were written in block capitals but they were as sure as they could be that James had penned then.

"If those letters are anything to go by, it is not beyond the bounds of possibility." Jack's tone was carefully neutral, as it had been for several days. Ruth sighed. Whatever he was feeling, he was not going to show it. He was, she supposed, waiting for verbal forgiveness. He did not see that the last twenty-four years were proof enough of that.

They talked endlessly about James's development – looking for the first signs of any mental instability. Ruth got out the family photograph albums and looked through them. It had been a long time since she had done so. Their wedding pictures, professionally taken; the honeymoon;

crazy snaps of them individually and one or two taken by waiters or other tourists; Polly in traditional pose, naked on a rug; James in his pram with Polly in her first school uniform beside it. Then Simon. Placid, calm Simon. Family holidays captured on celluloid but not one picture of James smiling as broadly as his brother and sister.

"It seems another lifetime when they were small. Remember how you used to try to get Simon interested in football?"

Jack smiled weakly. "He always did prefer an oval ball." But Jack was proud that Simon played rugby for his university.

"James never had any hobbies, did he?"

"No." They were both thinking of their efforts to find something he would stick at and the time they were asked to come and see his headmaster because he believed James might be dyslexic. It was not just that he did not mix well, his English was peculiar at times. Later they realised he enjoyed playing around with words.

"Yes! Of course."

"Jack?" Ruth jumped as he slapped the arm of his chair.

"He does have a hobby of a sort. Word games and crosswords."

"Of course." There had been endless rows when he was sent to bed before he was bored with playing Scrabble with Polly or Ruth, both of whom he often beat. "But that's not what the police were thinking of."

"I know." But it was a relief to them both to know that James was not entirely without interests.

It seemed to Stella that too many things were going on

184

at once for her to fully comprehend. Rebecca seemed to have settled for the status quo and had been rewarded with a screwdriver to replace the TV plug but by the time Martin returned she had had time to put her thoughts in order and explain exactly what she expected. Perhaps it would have been better to have been as emotional with him as she had been with her daughter. The result was that he said he was sick of being treated like a child and he was going to stay with his friends. He refused to tell her which friends, or their address, but she was surprised not to have heard from him over the weekend. If these friends were living with parents they wouldn't want an extra teenager about the place.

On Monday evening he returned to collect some clothes and said he had a permanent place to live. He was sharing a flat and could afford the rent. His job as a trainee mechanic paid enough and Stella had been surprised when he was taken on because his subjects at school had been on the arts side. She had not wanted him to leave school but Martin had used his father's leaving as an excuse. She saw now that further education would probably have been wasted on him.

"Am I to know the address?"

Martin wrote it down begrudgingly and added the phone number as a feeling of pity for his mother made him wonder if she'd be all right without a male in the household.

When he had gone again Stella looked around and realised how much more space there would be. And one less to cook and clean for, she thought with relief.

And there was this business at work with Alice. At first she thought it was just more gossip, just something else for them to all get worked up about. But Jack had only been in and then only once, for an hour or so. Then there were rumours that the police were involved, which had been confirmed by a bulletin on the local radio station.

How different her life was from the time she was with Colin, she thought. She felt so much more than just someone's wife or mother now. At Winter's she was her own person. And, she had to admit, how much more alive she was beginning to feel. Already she sensed what freedom would be like. Another few years and Rebecca would be gone.

None of it was what she had envisaged for then when she started out: school, 'A' levels, university then marriage and she would be a contented grandmother. It had been a dream built around other people, and one which did not take into consideration variance from the prescribed course. Now, she realised with a smile, she was finally beginning to accept that the only life she had the freedom to control was her own. And that in itself was a freedom. She only had herself to answer to. The thought was faintly exciting . . .

Chapter Nine

It was Saturday but Alice neither knew nor cared. James had left the mug of water on the table beside her. With difficulty she could swing around, pick it up two-handed, and sip it. When it was empty she asked for it to be refilled but was not sure if he did so immediately. Time had lost all meaning.

At one point squally showers had hit the window, hail and rain combined. It sounded like machine gun bullets but did not make her jump. James did not stir either. He was an empty shell. "Food!" she demanded at some point when she fought to resurface from whatever depths she was sinking into.

He brought a plate of cream crackers, unbuttered. The dry crumbs stuck to the roof of her mouth. She left them there. It was some time before enough saliva had formed to loosen them.

"Larry, untie me."

James moved his head. For a split-second she believed he might respond. Instead he picked up the bottle containing a couple of inches of whisky and took a few swallows.

She felt no pain, even though there were weeping welts on her ankles. She was overwhelmed with gratitude when James carried her out to the bathroom again and freed her legs. Except she could not stand. It was ten minutes before she was able to communicate her needs, that James must lift her onto the lavatory.

They had both been in the same clothes for a week. Alice's hair stuck to her head in greasy strands and she had not washed since Sunday morning. When James lifted her she did not notice the stench of his unwashed body, on which sweat had dried, nor did she smell his rancid breath, because it was equal to her own.

Sometimes Alice thought she was on a different plane, her mind watching her body from a distance. Lucid thoughts crept in now and then: how James had told her Larry had been outside her flat that Sunday afternoon and had seen her returning with Keith after she had been to her parents'; that Larry had seen her taking Keith up to her flat. But Larry had said he would make it come right, that he would show him a way to have Alice to himself.

Alice closed her eyes. For two days she had slept more than she was awake. It would, she sensed, be pleasant to drift out of life in such a way.

DI Pearson clamped his large hand to the back of his head and raised two ginger eyebrows. "And you're telling me they didn't know?"

DC Monroe nodded. "He's of age and the information's confidential."

"But when you're living under their roof?"

James Winter's GP had confirmed that his patient had, on several occasions, been prescribed mild tranquilisers and then been sent to see a specialist. The psychiatrist had warned of the onset of psychosis or possibly schizophrenia, but as it had been recognised at an early stage, regular medication would probably keep it under control. He had prescribed the necessary dose and written a letter accordingly to James's GP.

It had taken some doing but Monroe had ascertained that the prescription had been filled. Whether James had actually taken the tablets was another matter, but he had not returned to the surgery for a repeat. "There's usually some side effects," Monroe continued, which was one explanation for the discontinuance of James's medication.

But Pearson wasn't listening. He now realised that what they were dealing with was an unknown quantity and he would need to get some advice from a professional.

When Ruth saw the car pull up she hurried to the door expecting good news.

"I'm sorry to trouble you again, Mrs Winter." In the comfortable lounge DI Pearson explained her son's condition. Ruth listened in horrified silence.

This time the questions were more persistent, more searching. He wanted to know every nuance of James's personality, all his likes and dislikes. Ruth told him about the word games.

Alice rolled awkwardly onto one side and summoned up enough energy to sit up. She was thirsty again. Weak and numb, her bound hands knocked the mug to the floor. It rolled a few feet and the water left a dark patch.

"Larry." The word was a whisper. "Larry." She kept trying. She could not see if he was asleep or drunk or even dead. Her tongue was sticking to her teeth. She had to risk it. She had to get a response. "James," she said.

He did not look up but he made a sound and flicked his hand in an impatient gesture.

Alice knew then there would be no more water.

An incident room had been set up. The Superintendent was taking it that seriously. The team working on the case were in an early morning discussion of what steps to take next.

The possibility that they were holed up in an hotel or guest house had virtually been ruled out. Someone would have to come in each day to clean the room, and the Winters did not own any other property. Local farmers had been asked to search their barns and outhouses and sheds but both Ruth Winter and her husband believed their son was not equipped for roughing it.

The few names and addresses in the book in James's desk had been checked. No one recorded was sheltering them.

"A caravan, sir, or a rented property; it's the only way."

But how could they check every rented flat, house or room? How could they check every holiday camp, caravan site and private property that was on a short term let? Of course they could, but how long would it take? And DI Pearson realised that James Winter, if he had rented somewhere, would have used another name. It was recognised that criminals, when choosing a pseudonym, often unconsciously, stuck with their real initials. But James Winter was not the average criminal; he was a sick man. However, his enjoyment of words was all they had to go on . . .

"I wish we'd never started this," DI Pearson said at the

end of the day. This anagram business was getting out of hand. Mrs Winter had rung up to suggest that if her son did change his name that was how he might have done it. But not even the computer could make anything passable out of James Winter.

The second time Liz cried was when she saw a smiling picture of Alice on the front page of the evening paper. It had been taken in the back garden last summer. Next to it was a less recent photograph of James, possibly four or five years old but recognisable all the same. Because of her state of mind, Liz had to read the article three times before she took in what it said. Anyone knowing the whereabouts of one or both of the above named was asked to come forward. Information would be treated in the strictest confidence. The name of the street where the Powells lived was included, but not the number. Ruth and Jack's address was given as simply Cedar House, but few people had not at least heard of it. Ruth smiled grimly. Winter's Confectionery Company even got a mention, probably because it employed so many people, but the publicity would do no harm. 'The father of the missing boy, Jack Winter, is the proprietor of the confectionery firm situated in Weslar Yard,' the article continued, before giving a few more brief details. Liz guessed it was padding, to fill up the paper. Presumably the two lines referring to James's interest in word games was there for the same reason, and it was suggested that he may have changed his name.

The police took a different view: everything in the article had been included for a reason. They knew how many weirdos, how many cranks were out there always ready and willing to come forward with false information or false admissions, but there were a great many people who genuinely wanted to help, and there were those who liked to put the police straight.

Walter Garrett was one such man . . .

Alice knew she was dying. If not soon, then eventually. No help was coming, that was obvious. If anyone was looking for her they would never find her here. Numbness had been replaced with a clarity of thought she was sure she had not possessed before. James had gone out to the kitchen some time ago and had not returned. "I hope he's dead," she said, just to hear the sound of a voice. "At least I will have outlived him." But he returned with a piece of dry bread in his hand. It was mouldy. Alice would have eaten it had she been offered any. With the return of consciousness came the pain, a continual throbbing in her ankles and wrists, tortured muscles, a painful bladder, and hunger gnawing at her stomach. She tried to picture her parents having their evening meal but she could not see their faces. Were they worried or did they think she was on holiday? Was she expected back yet? She did not know because she had no idea how long she had been there.

James muttered and swore. Words from the gutter which no longer offended her. He was not going to hurt her now, she doubted he knew of her existence any more. Despite the swelling and the agony, she wriggled her toes. If she thought she was capable of it she would have got up and, feet together, jumped across the room to find a knife with which to free herself in the kitchen but it was too much effort to even sit up. She lay, with the rough material of the settee chaffing her face.

* * *

192

"Don't take on so, Marg." Mr Green patted her awkwardly on the shoulder.

"I can't help it. I should've told them sooner what I suspected."

"They found out for themselves quick enough. It wouldn't have made any difference."

"I suppose not." Marg had told the police everything she could think of relating to Alice. Deep down she knew that Mr Green was right, that mentioning James might be responsible for those notes would not have counted for much because Alice had already been missing for four days before it had occurred to her. It was Alice's safety she was crying for, not herself. With a decisive movement, she pulled a tissue from the sleeve of her cardigan and blew her nose. The supper had to be cooked, she had better get on with it. It was seeing the picture in the paper that had done it. She bent down to get a saucepan from the cupboard. Marg. Mr Green had called her Marg. She tutted, and pushed back the offending lock of hair. It must be getting to him, too, she thought as she chopped the cabbage with more force than was necessary.

Vera and Greg were coming over. It would hardly be a cosy foursome as she and Mr Green were not strictly a couple, but Marg and Vera felt closer to each other, needed each other in a peculiar sort of way because they had, initially been involved.

It's been harder on her, she thought, realising Vera was still officially convalescent. For six years Alice had worked with them, shared their jokes and the bad days. The balance was wrong without her youth and freshness.

"I'll pop out and get a bottle of sherry, shall I?" Mr Green offered.

"Sherry? You must be joking. Here." Marg pulled her purse out of her handbag and handed him a couple of notes. "Gin, a large bottle. And a litre of tonic. And something for yourself." She checked the fridge to make sure there was enough orange squash for her own mixer.

"There's no need." Mr Green thrust the money back into her hand, offended that she felt the need to offer to pay.

Marg mixed flour and suet and herbs for the dumplings and knew Mr Green already regretted his fleeting informality, in calling her Marg.

Walter Garrett could be nothing other than a retired colonel, so archetypal of the breed was he. Of medium height and corpulent build, the waistcoat he wore over his shirt, but without a jacket, stretched across his well-fed stomach. Thick, grey hair formed a fringe around his pate. It was neatly cut every fortnight. His voice was deep and loud. He was used to issuing commands and having them obeyed. It was a trait he carried over into his personal life, except, after he retired he realised Louisa was not the mouse he had taken her for. Louisa. He thought it was an inappropriate name for a colonel's wife but it was one thing he had not been able to alter. She kept their bungalow immaculate, he, likewise, the garden, the flowers as regimented as his men had been. He did not know that there were times when Louisa stopped herself from springing to attention when he entered a room, or that she sometimes did so, deliberately, behind his back with a salute worthy of any of his soldiers.

Yet they were accustomed to each other, comfortable and content. They had two things in common – one being the army: Louisa, despite her name, had been the ideal army wife, adept at organising bridge parties and dealing with the wives of the lower ranks. She had enjoyed having her housework and cooking done for her but was glad she was no longer young. It was a different world now.

Their second common bond was their addiction to word games. The quiet hours after dinner were ones they looked forward to because they did not believe in sitting around during the day with crossword puzzles. Walter tackled the *Times* crossword every day, meticulously timing himself. Louisa usually stuck to one of her books containing puzzles from previous newspapers. Sometimes she read. Once a week they played Scrabble, a tight, closed-in game, as they were good at the technique and had a long-memorised knowledge of allowed two-letter words. Louisa never let on that sometimes, sensing his mood, she let Walter win because he had a tendency to sulk. To her, playing the game was *really* all that mattered.

Walter read the evening paper with his pre-dinner drink. Another ritual that formed part of their lives. Now that she had a kitchen that was properly her own, Louisa had learned that she enjoyed cooking.

They ate in the dining room because Walter did not believe in sloppiness. "It's a downward slope to the devil," he was fond of saying.

"Um, jolly nice. That butcher does you proud," he said that evening. It was as near a compliment as she could hope for. "Seen this?" He pushed the paper across the table. "Damned fool girl's gone and got herself abducted."

Louisa took no notice of the way her husband's remark was phrased. She was used to him, he meant nothing against the girl.

195

"Police. Fools if you ask me."

"Why's that, dear?"

Walter pointed with his knife. "Got to be something in there. If what they're suggesting's true, that is. Why else bother to print it? Information's no good on its own."

"You mean they want the general public to work out what he might be calling himself?"

"Yes. It's not like the army in war time, they're not putting this out as deliberate misinformation to confuse the enemy."

"Pudding? Or are you full?"

"Cheese will be fine, not too much." Walter went to the sideboard where there was a supply of pens and paper and took out a notepad and biro. Louisa cleared the table and came back with celery, strong Cheddar which crumbled and stung the tongue, and some water biscuits.

She watched him for a second or two then asked for a sheet of paper, the dishes, with this new conundrum to solve, temporarily forgotten.

"Aha."

"Have you found something?" Louisa was surprised, she had fiddled around with the name James Winter but had come up with nothing that made any sense.

"Indeed, I have, my dear. Indeed I have. The police, as I said, are fools."

Louisa tried to hide her feeble attempt, anagrams were not her strong point, but Walter reached for it. She had changed tack and got as far as making Celia out of Alice. "Not bad, you were going along the right lines."

High praise indeed, but Walter had got there first. He could afford to be charitable.

"What do you think she's doing right now?" Vera glanced

196

at the clock encased in its wooden frame on Marg's mantlepiece. It was ten-fifteen on Saturday evening.

"She'll be all right."

Mr Green had not said much during the course of the evening, letting the women do all the talking. Greg had tried to engage him in conversation but knew nothing about fishing and did not realise Hilary Green was a little intimidated by a man who wore a suit to work. He had the sense to spot that Vera and Marg could not keep off the subject because talking about it was, in a way, cathartic, and from things Vera said, he was aware of how close they were. He also had one eye on the gin bottle which was rapidly emptying. Greg had brought some wine to go with the meal but they had forgotten to open it. He drank it now. It was too soon to push Vera over a decision. When she was completely well was the time, not when she was vulnerable and might agree for the wrong reasons, and this Alice thing wasn't helping.

Later, just as Mr Green seemed to be warming to him and it was time to leave, they had a quiet word and decided they would both take their women off somewhere for the day tomorrow. Greg had seen the tiredness in Vera's face and insisted they go home.

Vera let them into the flat. "Are you staying?"

"No. You're shattered. Get some sleep and I'll pick you up about eleven and we'll go out somewhere."

"OK." He saw she was relieved. He knew it would take longer than she anticipated before she was totally fit again.

"Anywhere special you'd like to go?"

"No. You choose. Greg, about what you were saying, about us living together."

"Yes?" He held his breath. Vera did not take kindly

to grand displays of emotion or affection, whichever way she had decided he would have to abide by it.

"I think it might work, no, wait. I can't do anything yet. If Alice is safe, I'll move in with you."

"If Alice is safe?" He did not understand. Was she peculiarly superstitious?

"I know it might sound daft, but I can't explain it."

"I'll do whatever you want." He kissed her with more passion than he meant to show, then left.

But in a way Vera could explain it. Alice had become a sort of talisman. If anything happened to Alice it was a sign that she and Greg were not meant to be together. Deep down she knew it was more than that. Why should Vera Langford, who had had so many men, so many chances, have a final stab at happiness when someone like Alice ended up in James's hands?

"There's still no news," Marg said on Monday morning before Jack came in. He might not come in at all, they had hardly seen him the previous week. "I keep thinking about what her family's going through. I'd be out of my mind, despite what I say about my lot."

"How many children do you have, Marg?"

"Three," she told Stella.

"And enough bloody grandchildren to start a football team," Vera added. "You've got a couple, haven't you?"

"Yes. A girl and a boy. The boy's just left home."

"There you are, that's one out of the way," Marg told her.

Stella frowned at Marg. "Is that how you felt?"

"Of course. Doesn't everybody? Don't worry, they'll keep coming back, when they want something or when they're in trouble."

It was a relief to hear it. Friends from the old days who had children older than her own spoke of their offspring as if they were angels, praising their achievements and saying how lucky they were. Thinking about Jack Winter she wondered how much of it had been true, if it was all an act to prove that their way of life was best.

"Jack's here." Vera nodded towards the office where they could see his back. A cloud of smoke obscured his head as he lit a cheroot. He turned, nodded at them and came down the stairs.

"You can stop for a moment, ladies, there's something I want to tell you before you hear it on the news. And when I've told you there's something I want you to consider. Not now, not necessarily today. You'll see what I mean when you've had time to think about it."

He led the way into the canteen and suggested someone made coffee. Marg and Vera lit up. If Stella was so keen to join them, she could see to the coffee.

Marg drew deeply on her cigarette. By the look of Jack's face the news wasn't good.

DI Pearson and his superiors were following every lead, however insignificant it appeared. From a neighbour opposite the house where Alice lived they had received confirmation that James's car had been parked outside at ten-thirty on the previous Saturday morning and that a few minutes later Alice had got into it. The car had been driven south, the direction which led to the town centre. But Pearson doubted they were anywhere in the town.

Instinct told him Alice was still alive. If she wasn't, James would not stay put, he would want to distance himself. But his car hadn't been sighted, recently, suggesting he was still holding her somewhere, rather than on the move. "Who?" he said into the telephone. "Put him on."

He listened for several minutes and as he did so, assessed that the man wasn't a crank and realised that what he said fitted. "Thank you, sir. We're always grateful for assistance from the public."

He looked down at the paper on which he had been writing. It might not mean anything but the name Larry Dawes was definitely an anagram of Weslar Yard, where Winter's confectionery was sited.

"We might end up a laughing stock, but get it circulated to the nationals," Pearson's superintendent told him. "There's always a chance the old buffer's right and someone might have dealt with a Larry Dawes recently. In fact, give them the whole story if they want it. Upsetting for the parents, but better that than a dead victim."

James was asleep. This time she was certain because she could hear his low snoring. The whisky bottle, another one, was on the floor beside him yet she sensed he was not drunk. He had only been sipping it and not very often.

Staring out of the window she could still see the room in her mind: Turkish-style rugs, chintz coverings and curtains, the table and chairs, a small bookcase, the contents of which she had not had a chance to look at. Would she be able to read if she roused James sufficiently to fetch her one? A long, narrow table up against the far wall with two drawers and a shelf beneath them. The fireplace, with its sooted interior and the chimney stack, its bricks darker around the edge from the smoke.

But out of the window there were living things. And freedom. Could she really get through another night?

Frustration and boredom and pain made her want to scream. To start and never stop until James killed her and put her out of her misery. If only he would talk to me, she thought, say something. Anything. She knew she had spoken aloud once or twice and wondered if she was becoming as mad as he was.

"Hold on, would you repeat that?" DI Pearson felt a surge of adrenalin. A counterpart from the Thames Valley Police was on the line and would be faxing the information through straight away. "John McNeil. Where is he now?" It was Sunday morning.

John McNeil was in Oxford where he was undertaking some research. It would take him six months at least, he had said, and therefore, because he was on a basic salary for that period, had decided to let out his cottage. He had seen the piece in the paper by chance, because, he said, if a name or a detail was familiar it tended to jump out of the page at you.

A man called Larry Dawes had rented his cottage. It had been too good an opportunity to miss. Dawes, he said, had seen his advert, responded at once and paid three months rent in advance, in cash, and had not been in the least concerned that the contract was not renewable.

McNeil agreed he had been an idiot not to take up references but the sooner things were sorted out, the sooner he had been able to begin his research, he explained. His presence, he was told, was not required at the cottage but he would be kept informed.

John McNeil went back to his lodgings. He was not a mercenary man but if his tenant was some sort of criminal the three months rent would no doubt be forgotten and he could re-let the place. There were always enough ghouls who would be prepared to stay at the scene of a crime. He shrugged his shoulders and hoped the girl would be all right and that his property had not been damaged.

Alice had once read a book about American Indians. For some reason it came into her mind. Certain tribes, she recalled, starved themselves until they hallucinated and then their tribal name would come to them in their trance-like state. James was in that state, although whether from hunger, drink or madness she did not know. It was her own hallucinations which bothered her. She was, literally, starving.

Out of the window she had seen something but she did not know what it was, only that she had not seen it before. Half an hour later she saw it again and believed it might be nearer. It was nothing more than a minute glint which might not be real. She had experienced flashing and squiggles in front of her eyes, before.

It didn't matter. Nothing mattered. She closed her eyes again.

And then she heard a voice.

It wasn't James's voice and it wasn't real, of course. She laughed. It was faint, cracked sound. James had said he wanted her with him, well she was about to join him in whatever world he inhabited.

Then there was banging and a shout and James stumbled towards the front door. He tried to open it but it was locked. There was a crash and the doors and window frames rattled.

"James has gone away," she heard him say.

Then another voice: "It's all right. Everything's going to be all right."

"Yes," she said, and smiled because it was all part of

the game, all part of the madness into which she had entered.

In the whole of his career, DI Pearson had never been more relieved than when this case was over. There had been marksmen and people specially trained for persuading hostage-takers into setting their victims free, and the whole rigmarole. And none of it had been needed. With telescopic lenses it was apparent that James Winter was in no state to put up any resistance. He thanked God that he was not the one who would have had to make the decision of whether to go in.

An officer had kicked in the back door and handcuffs were on James Winter's wrists before he knew what had hit him. And the girl was alive. Another success story. DI Pearson's promotion looked certain.

Alice thought she had heard her mother's voice, but when she opened her eyes there was no one there. Hours must have passed because the sun was at a different angle, a ray from somewhere making the thin blue veins in her hands stand out. She must have slept again because it was night. Now there was a small light illuminating the room, not the sun, and she realised she was in a bed. When she moved a hand she felt a prick. Something was attached to it. "Keep still, it's an intravenous infusion, a drip," the nurse amended. "Instead of food."

Alice tried to sit up but everything hurt. Her hands were not secured, neither were her feet. Gently and quietly the nurse explained that she was in hospital, in a private room and that her parents would be back soon but she must try to sleep again.

Alice didn't believe her, but the bed was comfortable so she closed her eyes.

Liz Powell reapplied her make-up for the fourth time.

When Derek had opened the door to the policeman some time during Sunday afternoon she had feared the worst. Items of her daughter's clothing had been removed from her flat – Liz had supplied the spare key – for use by tracker dogs.

Derek, assuming the same as his wife, had led the man into the living room, knowing he would be unable to bear hearing the news on his own. It had taken several seconds before they realised the man was smiling and that, for him, it made a change to be the bringer of good news.

Derek put his arms around Liz and they stood, unspeaking, tears running down both their faces. "Where is she?" Liz finally asked.

"On her way to hospital. She hasn't been harmed," he added quickly, "but she needs food and rest and they'll have to examine her. Just to make sure." He saw what was going through the parents' minds. "There's a car outside, we'll run you up there."

They arrived first. The forty-five minutes it took for Alice to arrive by ambulance seemed like a lifetime. "Alice." Liz stepped forward but Derek put a restraining hand on her arm.

"Let them do what they have to first, love."

She was taken away on a trolley, unaware of their presence.

"You're not stopping me this time!" Vera told Greg jubilantly, on Monday night. Jack had come in to the factory, but only briefly, to impart the news that Alice and James had been found. It had been kept quiet until Monday to prevent the press swarming all over the hospital or pestering the families. Marg and Vera's pleasure was tempered with the knowledge of what must be going through Jack's mind.

"He looks bloody awful," Vera said. "What'll happen to James?"

Marg assumed he would be sent to some psychiatric hospital, but she didn't really know. What she did know was that the two of them would be out on the town tonight and never mind that there was work in the morning.

"Don't be too late," Greg warned her.

"Greg, stop it, you're beginning to sound like a nagging wife. And if . . ." She did not continue but turned to face the mirror to put on the dangling diamanté ear-rings which matched her necklace.

Before she left she looked up the Powells' home telephone number in the directory and rang it, but there was no reply. She guessed where they would be.

The landlord in The Unicorn gave them their first drink on the house as his part of the celebration. The women from the factory weren't a bad bunch and they always used the place for their evenings out or a starting base for their outings. He had missed them lately, with Vera being out of action and then Alice. However, by the look of them things were back to normal tonight. Good old Marg was resplendent in a purple satin tunic with silver embroidery around the neck, worn over a black skirt. And she's still got a neat pair of ankles he thought, taking a surreptitious look as he wiped down the bar counter. Her heels were nearly as high as Vera's.

He was a pragmatic man. Alice's abduction had been a bit of excitement for a while but people soon forgot.

Alice would probably get over it in time; it was Jack Winter he felt sorry for.

"Thank God," Ruth said. "Thank God he hasn't harmed her."

They did not at first know the extent of their son's illness. Gradually it became apparent, the signs had been there, they just hadn't seen them.

James was being held in custody, more because he might be a danger to himself than for what he had done, and the police were awaiting psychiatric reports.

"You did the right thing," Ruth said, when Jack told her he was footing the bill for a private room for Alice. Under the circumstances he would have done the same, even if Alice had not been his daughter. It was their son who had been responsible for putting her there.

A little of the old brashness had disappeared, but Jack would survive. The main thing was it was over, and Ruth knew he would see that James had the best care possible. If he came home to them at some point in the future they would ensure he took whatever medication he was prescribed. "They're always a worry, aren't they?" she said wistfully, realising that no matter how old children became, parents still felt a sense of responsibility towards them. How much worse for Jack when two of his had been missing. She wondered if, through recent events, Derek had been made aware of the true circumstances of Alice's birth. If he hadn't, Ruth would not be the one to tell him, enough damage had been done.

Jack stood in his spot by the French windows. He would offer Alice a chance of leaving with a couple of months wages which he could put down as redundancy pay but he would also tell her she was welcome to stay.

But what about the other women? Vera, Marg and Stella had also suffered because of his son's illness. How would they feel about continuing to work for Winter's? Only one way to find out, he decided, I'll ask. "I'm going in for an hour or so. Are you all right?" he asked Ruth.

"I'm fine, Jack. When do you suppose they'll let us see James?"

"When he's stable, I suppose." He kissed her as he always did before he left the house. Yes, she's going to be fine, he thought as he got into the car. And when he had sorted things out at the factory he would try to make it up to her.

Alice wanted to go home but the hospital insisted she stay another night. She had answered so many questions she was exhausted and wanted the peace of her old bedroom in her parents' house. It was forty-eight hours before she was convinced she was safe. The drip had been removed and she was able to eat, but only small amounts; soup and ice-cream to start with. There were bandages around her ankles but there had been enough give in the bindings around her wrists that dressings were unnecessary.

"Do I smell?" was one of the first questions Alice had asked when she was aware it really was Liz sitting by the bed.

Liz had laughed because it was a good sign. She had been warned there might be difficulties, post traumatic stress, but Alice was not displaying any of the symptoms. "No," she said, "you were given a bed bath."

"How did they find me, Mum?"

Liz outlined the details telling her that it was all down to a crossword freak but Alice was unable to take it in. The main thing was that James could do her no more

207

harm. Around Alice's bed were flowers from Marg, Vera and Stella – but nothing from Jack. Liz wondered if he was too embarrassed to make contact. Having Alice back was all that had mattered but now she was safe she was able to reflect how lucky it was that Derek need never know her true parentage.

After three days at home Alice was getting used to being able to walk around the house, to make tea or a sandwich whenever she felt like it, which was quite often. But decisions needed to be made. There was the question of work. Jack had called in the previous evening and put forward his proposal.

"I'm not coming back," she told him. "Not just because of what's happened. I needed a change anyway. It's been fun, and I'll miss the others but . . ."

"But you want a bit more out of life?"

"Yes."

"And you'll accept my offer?"

Three months wages would be welcome. It would give her a chance to recover fully and the time to make careful plans. She would accept it, but nothing more. Jack's offer to help finance her course was generous but hardly appropriate for a man who was merely her employer.

Liz did not intervene; it was Alice's life, but she was pleased by her refusal, the tie between herself and Jack would finally be broken.

The news was soon stale. Local reporters came to the door and Alice gave them a brief interview and once more her picture was in the paper then other events took priority. Marg and Vera came to see her but after two weeks she knew it was time to go back to the flat.

"Not yet," Liz said. "Give yourself a bit more time." But Alice was adamant.

The evening before she left Keith called round. He had waited until the fuss had died down, knowing she would be inundated with visitors. Alice thanked him for the flowers he brought and they sat drinking coffee, just as they used to, but many things had changed. They chatted companionably but the spark was no longer there. It hadn't been there on her part for months, of course, but now she could say the same of Keith.

"How's Jackie? Are you still seeing her?"

"Yes."

"Serious?" She smiled.

"I think so."

"What does Joan make of it?"

Keith shrugged and and grinned. "I haven't asked her." But he did not tell her of the harsh words that had been necessary. "I think she might come over herself later."

"OK?" Liz asked when Keith had gone, worried that he might have upset her.

"Absolutely."

On Saturday morning Derek drove Alice back to her flat. She had not been inside it since the day James had taken her to the cottage. Liz had collected clothes for her. It looked different, yet familiar, and smelled a bit musty because the windows had not been opened. On the table were more flowers and a large box of chocolates, not produced by Winter's, and a note. '*Sweets for my Sweet*,' it said, '*Love Mum and Dad.*'

Alice hugged him and felt the tears. It would pass, she knew that, but every now and then they came for no reason. There were also several envelopes on the

209

table, one of which was from the college where she had written for details of the beautician's course. She slit it open with a thumbnail and looked through it. Enclosed was an application form. Her mind was made up.

Josie came up later that evening, bearing wine and a Chinese take-away. She had been to see Alice in hospital but she was sleeping at the time.

"It's only because my lovely solicitor is away. You do realise you're second best."

It was refreshing after all the solicitous attention to be in Josie's company.

"If you're up to it, fancy the cinema tomorrow?"

"I'm up to anything now. And look, I've taken your advice." She showed her the completed application form.

"Good for you, girl. When do you start?"

"I've got to be accepted first."

"You will be."

And she was.

The next few months passed faster than she had anticipated. Jack's money was in the bank but it was not long before boredom set in. Alice took a part-time job in a shop just for something to do. She enjoyed it, being amongst people again, but this time there would be no getting involved, no taking the easy option. She had made it quite clear that she would be leaving on a certain date.

As the time drew nearer Liz took her shopping. "My treat," she said. "Your Dad's had a rise, it was his idea. Besides, you want to look the part. And you need something for Vera's wedding."

Alice had been surprised at the news, her own having eclipsed everything else for several weeks, but she was able to detect a trace of uncertainty. "God, I hope I'm

210

doing the right thing," Vera said on more than one occasion.

"You've got shot of two before. You can always do the same again if it doesn't work out. Go on, live dangerously," was Marg's philosophical contribution. And the register office wedding, a small affair, was in a week's time.

"Just look at the state of her." Marg nodded towards Vera waiting in the reception area of the Town Hall. She was visibly shaking. But Alice thought how nice she looked in a plain suit. It was Marg who looked more like the bride in a white dress with a ruffle from neck to waist and a floppy, white straw hat with a navy ribbon.

It should have been me, Alice thought, realising that she would have been a married woman of almost three months. And I'm so glad it isn't. Different for Vera who, whatever she said, needed a man, and whose life would never change. And if anyone could, it would be Greg who made her happy.

Mr Green was looking uncomfortable in a suit, tugging at his collar and checking with Marg that his tie was straight. "No one's going to look at you," she told him firmly. "Stop fussing." Alice was the only one without a partner although the invitation had included a guest. There was no one she wanted to bring and she enjoyed being on her own.

The ceremony was over in less than fifteen minutes. "Seems to get quicker every time."

"Honestly Vera." Marg was disapproving: hardly tactful words from the new Mrs Rawlins. Greg did not seem to mind, his smile was bemused as if he suddenly realised what he'd taken on.

211

They went from the Town Hall to a restaurant. There were ten of them and Jack had insisted on paying for the champagne. The other women had chipped in for a wedding present, he had said that the booze would be his. Alice took a sip then looked at the bottle. It was an unwelcome reminder, the same kind and vintage as James had offered her. What the hell, she thought. This was Vera's day and James was getting treatment at some expensive clinic somewhere miles away. Marg had kept her informed. She swallowed half a glassful.

When it was over they saw Greg and Vera off. They were flying to Spain on a night flight and had to go home for their cases.

"Well, my girl, now the formalities are over, how about a proper drink down The Unicorn? Champagne's all right, but like I always say, you can't beat a gin and orange. You carry on. I'll see you later," Marg added to Mr Green whose face had dropped at the thought of more socialising and more drink.

Marg and Alice walked up the High Street in their finery. Alice had chosen a yellow and green floral skirt, a muted lime green vest and a linen jacket in the same colour. As an outfit it was smart but she could wear the pieces individually afterwards.

"Number three, was it?" the landlord inquired, realising what the occasion had been. "Pity you're not thinking of remarrying, Marg." He winked.

"Cheeky bugger. Anyway, you've got a wife."

"Indeed I have, and a lovely woman at that." He turned and smiled at the thin, grim-faced woman who had just come out of the kitchen. "I was just saying . . ." but she had sniffed distainfully and retreated to the steak and kidney pies which were about to

212

go into the oven for the following day's lunchtime trade.

"You will keep in touch, won't you, Alice? It's not the same without you," Marg said.

"Of course I will." Alice sipped her drink. Yes, for a time they would meet, like in the old days, but it would be her replacement who would become part of the group, herself an outsider, no longer able to join in or appreciate the jokes, no longer able to share their disappointments and problems. There would be letters, and occasional telephone calls and eventually they would peter out when they no longer had anything to say to one another. And it was best that way. A new life was supposed to be just that, not clinging to the past like a frightened child clings to its mother. Alice looked at Marg and saw in her eyes that she, too, knew it would be that way, but for now they would enjoy each other's friendship. "Another?"

"I should think so." Marg had been staring at her empty glass long enough for Alice to take the hint.

"Jack was very good about all that business," Marg remarked.

"Oh?"

"He said he wouldn't be upset if we wanted to leave and offered to give us a month's money and good references. Where would we go, though, Alice, Vera and me? And Stella, come to that. I'm too long in the tooth for change. Besides, Jack's a decent man; he's taken it hard. I envy you, though, everything out there waiting for you. Still, I've got a bit of company in Mr Green. Hilary," she added laughing.

And suddenly Alice saw the sadness behind the words, saw how she could have become, trapped in a rut until it was too late to do anything about it, or possibly like Vera, on an endless search for perfection. A wave of

213

relief made her limp. There was so much to look forward to.

The date for her departure arrived. Alice sat in her flat which now contained only the landlord's furniture. Her own belongings were stored at her parents' house and her case was at her feet as she waited for the taxi which would take her to the station. All that was left was to leave the key on the table and shut the door behind her.

She stood up and took a final look in the mirror; blue jeans, a white T-shirt and a black, studded belt emphasised her slimness, although she had quickly regained the weight she had lost during that nightmare of a week. Some inner strength had kept her going, she realised that now, and it would keep her going in the future, if the course became difficult or she started missing her friends. There would be new friends, boyfriends and her own achievements to look forward to. And then a career.

The future was beginning now, in these last few moments in her flat. Alice had promised to keep in touch with Josie, and she intended doing so. She had a feeling it was a friendship that would last.

She heard the toot of a horn and placed the key on the table and slammed the door behind her. The taxi driver put her case in the boot. "Where to, love?"

"The railway station, please."

"Going anywhere nice?"

"Oh, yes," she answered, without elucidating.

Only when she was on the train, in her reserved seat with a table, did the enormity of it hit her. She laughed softly. The woman opposite gave her a funny look then went back to her newspaper.

Alice was free. Free from Keith and James and work and family. It did not really matter what the future held, all that mattered was that she was an independent woman.

"You'll miss her, won't you?" Ruth asked her husband.

"I will, Ruthie, I have to admit it."

"Well, look on the bright side," she said briskly. "She'll do well and you'll be able to say seventy-five per cent of your children, instead of only fifty per cent have made something of themselves."

"Ruth!" he said to her retreating back, then closed his mouth because it was one of the rare occasions she had left him speechless.